D0701434

THE MAN BACK THERE

The Man Back There

and

Other Stories

Winner of the 2007
Mary McCarthy Prize
in Short Fiction
Selected by Mary Gaitskill

by David Crouse

Sarabande  Books
LOUISVILLE, KENTUCKY

© 2008 by David Crouse

FIRST EDITION

All rights reserved

No part of this book may be reproduced without written permission of the publisher. Please direct inquiries to:

Managing Editor
Sarabande Books, Inc.
2234 Dundee Road, Suite 200
Louisville, KY 40205

Library of Congress Cataloging-in-Publication Data

Crouse, David.
    The man back there and other stories / by David Crouse. — 1st ed.
        p.   cm.
    "Winner of the 2007 Mary McCarthy Prize in short fiction, selected by Mary Gaitskill."
    ISBN 978-1-932511-63-5 (pbk. : alk. paper)
    I. Title.
    PS3603.R685M36 2008
    813'.6—dc22   2007043760

Cover image by Nancy Diessner, provided courtesy of the artist

Cover and text design by Charles Casey Martin

Manufactured in Canada
This book is printed on acid-free paper.

Sarabande Books is a nonprofit literary organization.

THE KENTUCKY ARTS COUNCIL

The Kentucky Arts Council, a state agency in the Commerce Cabinet, provides operational support funding for Sarabande Books with state tax dollars and federal funding from the National Endowment for the Arts, which believes that a great nation deserves great art.

For Melina, with much love,
and Dylan, in your second year

CONTENTS

ACKNOWLEDGMENTS

Some of these stories first appeared in slightly different form in the following publications: *The Beloit Fiction Journal*: "The Man Back There," "The Forgotten Kingdom" (as "Warriors of the Forgotten Kingdom"), and "The Observable Universe"; *The Sonora Review*: "What We Own"; *Chelsea*: "Posterity" (as "The Long Run"); *Arts & Letters*: "Dear"; *The Greensboro Review*: "The Castle on the Hill"; *Quarterly West*: "Show and Tell" (as "Time Capsule"); and *Salamander*: "Torture Me."

I would like to thank Frank Soos, for his wise advice and kindness; Nancy Diessner, for being a kindred spirit and good friend; Jenny Barber, Rusty Dolleman, Derick Burleson, Amanda Bales, Stuart Ste. Croix, Jessica Ste. Croix, Russ van Paepeghem, Gerri Brightwell, Kyle Mellen, and Sarah Gorham, for reading my work with sensitivity and care; and especially my parents, Alfred and Marie Crouse, for their support throughout the years.

ix

FOREWORD

I CHOSE THESE STORIES BECAUSE THEY MADE ME FEEL. This is a very subtle and subjective thing to explain. The characters featured are ordinary people, sometimes living lives that are somewhat more dull or deprived than we might like to consider ordinary: bereaved, rejected, alone enough and poor enough that the random objects in someone else's old coat pocket are of great material and imaginative interest. The situations they confront are generally pretty ordinary too, or have become ordinary to them: a man punches a guy in a bar after an insult to a girlfriend of a few months; two little boys explore the forbidden closet of a disappeared and possibly dead older brother; a divorced dog-catcher, hungry and at work on a cold Thanksgiving, decides to crash his ex-wife's dinner party after hearing about the murder of two children he's glimpsed earlier in the day—bringing along a dog he's about to put down. These situations are not perceived dramatically by the characters or rendered so by the author. Yet they each carry the seeds of dramatic anguish, anger, self-doubt, and the mystery of how opposing emotions can suddenly connect. At some point in each story, these seeds may fiercely sprout; the character may be aware of this, or partially aware, or simply feel a dim, puzzling disturbance that he experiences as a question with an answer just out of reach.

If I wanted, I could say some of these things about the other collections I read for Sarabande. Small, poignant situations are the traditional purview of the short story, and underdogs are always popular. But while many of the other collections were very well-observed, intelligent, and precise, they didn't ultimately make me feel to the degree that *The Man Back There* makes me feel. By "feel" I don't mean that I felt a particular emotion, I mean that the outcome of almost every story here mattered to me. I *felt* the characters like I would feel a stranger in a room or on a bus with me, that is, with an irrational sympathy more animal than moral in its nature. Right after the man punches his girlfriend's ex in a bar, he feels both her unspoken excitement and unspoken fear. They are standing around outside the bar and she is wearing his coat. He wants to go to the lake to look at the moon and she doesn't. Is it because: "She had found his knife in his pocket too—he could tell from the thoughtful expression, the way she tilted her head down and away from him—and maybe the breath mint from the restaurant they had gone to last week, or the thimble he used when playing guitar, his mother's thimble, with which she had made sweaters and blankets and little dolls with buttons for eyes." We don't know her response any more than he does, but we sense it in the movement of her head—as we sense the jumbled, humble individuality of his life by running our minds, like fingers, over the contents of his pocket. Couples keep coming out of the bar and the narrator looks anxiously to see if "the man back there" will emerge. At one point, he notes: "The door opened behind them again." It has a subtle double meaning: the door to a past he has complex feelings about has opened, too. The complexity of his response is based in part on principle, but also on his animal nature, and on emotions he doesn't fully understand—and who among us can claim to fully know our own emotions?

In "Show and Tell" a little boy wants to poke his expressionlessly bereaved playmate with a sharp toy, to see a grimace of pain, or even just a flinch: "... it would've been like a gift." This "gift" would enable him to return a broken toy he has stolen and uniquely repaired, a gift he is longing to give. Instead, he'll "have to be satisfied with this odd balance, this double withholding." But of course he isn't satisfied at all. Is the kid sad and mean? Yes. But he's also alive and questing with his mixed urges and his efforts to put them together. Like the man waiting outside the bar, we share his bluntly felt confusion acutely. We want it to be clarified, and we know it can't be, at least not right away, as the characters would like. Yet we feel heartened and somehow satisfied just to see that the author has revealed it so deeply and so well. In this revelation we glimpse, with the author, a mind bigger than ours, maybe God, maybe something without a name, that sees, understands, and forgives even when we cannot.

—MARY GAITSKILL

THE MAN BACK THERE

AFTER THE FLASH OF WILD MOTION—after the thrown drink, the
tumbling chair as Sweets jumped to his feet and ducked his head,
after Sharon's near-fall as he shoved her toward the exit—they stood
on the sidewalk without speaking.

Sweets took off his coat and wrapped it around her shoulders. It
had grown cold—they could see their breath—and he wanted to
comfort her, but he didn't want to hold her.

She jammed her hands down into the broken-buttoned pockets
of the jacket and looked back at the door. She was probably expecting
it to open, and for the man to charge out and then up the stone steps,
his face wet from Sharon's White Russian. But Sweets guessed he
was probably not even off the floor; and even if he was, he was
probably just talking to his friends, twisting the story around as fast
as he could, making it his own. *Crazy people. Did you see them hightail
it out of here? This town is full of crazy people.*

As he looked across the road at the fire-scarred mill building,
Sweets imagined the river the building obscured as it slid past his life
on its way from the White Mountains to the Atlantic. The moon was
full and it had rained lightly about an hour ago and people were
coming outside just to take a look around.

The bar was packed anyway, which was probably part of the
reason what had happened had happened—too many people

bumping shoulders. "We should get out of here," he said, but they didn't move except to step closer together.

"Smoke?" someone said. A slump-shouldered guy smiling at something invisible. He wanted a cigarette, and then he probably wanted to talk about the Red Sox, who had just won seven of their last eight games. Sweets told him no, because his cigarettes were in the pocket of the coat Sharon was wearing, and the smoker nodded a quick *Thanks anyway* and smiled over at Sharon, who looked down at the sidewalk. She seemed smaller in the coat, almost childlike, especially with her hair tied back. She had old eyes, yes, but a young face, like the innocent, determined faces of the high school girls he sometimes saw running in the late afternoon, in clusters of three or four. They seemed almost weightless, to be running like that, toward his truck, then gone.

"I bet it looks really nice down by the water," Sharon said.

His hand hurt, his two middle fingers just above the knuckle. He hoped it wasn't anything serious. It had been six months since he had insurance, a year since he had been to a doctor, three for a dentist. He was forty-four years old last month, and sometimes he worried that his teeth were going bad in his head, or a dark spot was growing on his lung or heart or other more mysterious organ. He tightened his fingers into a fist. Sharon saw him do it and she glanced away.

"Yeah, well," Sweets said. "It'd look prettier out by the lake."

The bar door opened and two people stepped outside—a man and a woman, his hand around her waist. Their heads turned in Sweets' general direction and recognition crossed their faces, or was it just the cold and drizzle that made them frown? Sweets tried to hold their eyes with his own, as if to say, *We've got nothing to be ashamed of,* but they turned their gazes on each other. Then they brushed past him and sauntered across the street.

He watched them go. They separated to move around a telephone pole, and then came back together in some simple little choreography. They were drunk and possibly in love, and they were still laughing as they moved around the corner and out of sight.

We need to get out of here, Sweets thought, and then it occurred to him that if his hand hurt as much as it did, then the man might be in serious pain; the thought filled him with an odd sense of pride and shame, and he remembered his own size. He was usually not conscious of his height, but he was a big man, a couple of inches over six feet. When he entered a room, he hunched slightly—almost shyly, Sharon had told him. She had been the one to point it out, in that affectionate, needling way she pointed out most of his quirks: the way he ate, head down, silent; the hair-trigger way he slept; and the fact that he owned next to nothing. "You could fit everything in this place into the back of my Civic," she had said once. His savings account had been stuffed with cash then from two months of work in a Gloucester cannery, and he had made a face and said, "Watch out. I just might buy a couch."

"You wouldn't have the guts," she had said back, and man, that had been it, the first time they had come together just right. He wondered if that was spoiled now, in some way he wouldn't understand until later.

That's where he had wanted to go tonight. The lake. He had a six-pack under the passenger's seat of his truck and a bed roll behind the seat and the pack of cigarettes in his coat, another in the glove compartment. It would have been a good night, but Sharon had wanted to be around people and really, who could blame her? She had spent all week in that cramped payroll office, and Sweets had been out in Tewksbury, helping a friend. Today, they had risen early and bled five pigs, four to sell and one, the largest, for the party tomorrow. His back ached from lifting, and from using the chainsaw the day before, and his mind was weary with all the talk—at lunch, at work, when driving from house to pens and back. At the end of the day, he had been too exhausted to even call her, so when he got back home tonight and Sharon said, "Want to come to town?" he figured, sure, why not?

"I'm pretty happy with this moon," she said. "I bet the one out at the lake is great, but you know what they say about gift horses."

She had found his knife in his pocket too—he could tell from the thoughtful expression, the way she tilted her head down and away from him—and maybe the breath mint from the restaurant they had gone to last week, or the thimble he used when playing guitar, his mother's thimble, with which she had made sweaters and blankets and little dolls with buttons for eyes. Stuff just kind of died there, in the pockets of that coat. Whenever he was trying to scrape money together, he always headed there first and found six or seven or sometimes twenty dollars. It seemed like luck when that happened.

"Hey," he said. "We should really get going."

The truck was parked on the other side of the street, and he was sober enough to drive it, although Sharon would probably disagree, and say something as he put the key in the ignition and turned her over. Not enough to stop him, and she had been drinking too, more than he had. If she hadn't downed the first two drinks so quickly, she wouldn't have thrown the third, and he wouldn't have stepped in front of her and raised his arms like a boxer.

4

The man had been standing too, a beer bottle in his hand, and Sweets had known then it was a weapon—even though the man might not have known it yet that's what it would have become if Sweets had given him the chance. So Sweets raised his arms, knocked over his chair, and moved in like he was going to hug him. Then he and Sharon were heading toward the door, past the waitress, who Sweets knew. He would pay her the next time he saw her, over at the diner on Mechanic Street, where she worked her second job.

Sharon looked at him and nodded okay, but they didn't move an inch. "In a minute, I think," she said thoughtfully. "I'm still a little frazzled. So are you. Have you ever done anything like that before?"

"Not really," he said. "Sort of, though, I guess."

Today he had taken his knife and moved it across the pig's throat and felt the muscle jerk through his hand and palm like electricity. As unsentimental as he was about farm animals, it was always a little sad to kill something you had seen born. It was a reminder of his own mortality as much as the pig's, and of the funny way events trailed behind you like a shadow. So he gave the pig his solemnity and attention as compensation, and the pig died quickly, with little fanfare. Then they bent down and rolled it across the plastic tarp. This was the one they were keeping.

But it didn't happen like that, did it? So slow-mo and rational? Because Sweets had been angry, and he had disliked the man's beer-reddened face, the way he was performing for his friends, his expensive leather coat, and the way Sharon had said, when she first noticed him at the other end of the table, "Don't look, but there's that ex-boyfriend I told you about. The one who twisted my arm behind my back."

Right then, out there looking at the moon, Sweets could unravel the trail of events and make sense of it, lay it out in his head step by step, like he was giving directions to some out of the way place. But the more it slipped behind him, like a road, the more confusing it got. Had the man stood up first, or had it been Sweets? He remembered the man stumbling like he had been pushed, not punched. He didn't remember if there had been blood or not. There probably had been blood.

He looked back at the bar. Another couple was walking out. The woman was in her early thirties, about Sharon's age, and she looked like she didn't have a worry in the world. Sweets said, "Do you think he's okay?"

"He's a scumbag," she said. "I told you that. I told you the kind of things he did."

"Sure," he said. He had listened to her talk about many things, up there in his loft that smelled of wood and maple leaves and dog. She seemed to get unglued up there, after sex, and talked about her father and his angry moods, the silence in the house, her string of jobs and boyfriends; some of them had been very kind to her, but their kindness had an edge of deceit to it: other women, other plans, stinginess with affection, one eye on her and one eye elsewhere. The usual business.

Other men had been not-so-kind, like the one in the bar, who once had jerked her arm behind her back, pushed her against a wall, and told her to shut her damned mouth. Sweets remembered that, although he didn't remember *why* the man had done it—the story that went with the image of Sharon's face pressed against the eagle-print wallpaper of her kitchen pantry. He said, "How long have we known each other?"

He decided he didn't like her hands in his pockets. Fine, wear the coat, he thought, but keep your hands out of the pockets. She said, "About eight months if you want to count everything, you know?"

Sweets wondered what they were waiting for, if Sharon *wanted* to bump into her ex again. Maybe she wanted another scuffle.

He knew it was a weakness to even think those things about her. Hell, when it came down to it, maybe it was he who was waiting. But he had never been the kind of person who could fully control his dark impulses, and so he let the thoughts come, and then turn into words. "You think we know each other pretty well, huh?" he asked. He was getting cold now, because he was just wearing a T-shirt and jeans. He touched his palm to his ass to make sure he hadn't lost his wallet on the way to the door. There were two hundred dollars there from the farming, minus the bar tab he would pay up tomorrow or the next day.

"I don't know," she said. "I don't know about that."

Yes, he was cold, and he wanted a cigarette, and he wished he could remember more about what Sharon had said up there in the loft. He had been careless when listening to her.

They were walking to the truck now, her out front, him following. He wanted to keep walking, past the broken-down mill building, and just get a single look at the light on the river, but instead he fished around for his keys, and then realized she had them, in the coat. She gripped them in both hands and unlocked the door.

"Don't get mad at *me*," she said. "Just because you think you're a knight in shining armor. I don't tell you to do what you do, and I don't tell you to think what you think. That's your job."

He moved around to the passenger's side and she reached across and flipped open the door. He said, "I don't know what you're talking about."

She was the one who had waited to see another glimpse of what she had done, and she was the one who had thrown the drink when her ex had said, "You're fucking farmers now, huh, Sharon?" and sniffed the air like he could smell sheep and cows and manure and maybe their sex too, leftover from those nights in the loft. She started the truck and he said, "You're too drunk to drive. Let's switch places."

"Look at you," she said. "You're messed up. Your hands are shaking."

She gave him a cigarette from his coat and the lighter and he smoked it while the engine idled. He thought of kissing her, but the idea of it seemed impossible, and he tried to think instead of the next morning, when he would wake alone in the loft and have eight hours of sleep between himself and the punch he had thrown. He said, "Man, I am dog tired."

"Me, too," she said. "It's been a bruiser of a week."

The windows were fogging up. Sharon clicked the heater on and pulled the jacket off her shoulders and said, "Sometimes I wish I didn't have a history. You know how soap is when you unwrap it?"

Tomorrow, there would be a pig roast in Tewksbury, the carcass spread across a barrel Sweets had cut in half with a Saws-All that morning. He and Sharon would go together. She would be sitting on a stump, her body bent with the October cold, and Sweets would fix her a plate of potato salad and blueberry pie and long strips of barbecued pork. They would smile at each other as Sweets walked over. He could anticipate the moment like he could anticipate the taste of the food, the smell of the fire, the buzz from the beer. He wondered when he started living the future as hindsight.

Off to his right, behind the building, he knew there was moonlight on the river; he had swum there when younger, drunkenly shouting out to his wife on the shore. The current had taken him down to the box company, where he had scrambled ashore, and later, he had learned people had died doing exactly what he had done. At the time, it had felt good, though; it still felt good, in a way—his wife calling after him, angrily, wanting him back beyond all reason, so that it sounded like *she* was the one who was in danger of drowning.

"We should maybe take a shower together tonight," he said to Sharon, although there was no flirtation or desire in his voice. "Get the smoke off us."

They often showered and then spooned, their wet bodies forming one shape, her back against his stomach, his lips against her neck. It was as much for comfort as for lust, and she often slept through the night that way, almost motionless except for her feet, which shifted and kicked like she was learning to swim. She had said so much up there, and he had listened, and the listening itself had been an unburdening.

He felt sorry for the man in the bar now, for being in the wrong place at the wrong time. He probably didn't want to have a history either, right? He probably wanted that very much. He had slapped Sharon Heffernan twice with the back of his hand, and told her to shut-up, and wrenched her arm, and lied to her about a girlfriend he had in Lowell, and Sweets wondered if he had a place like the loft, where he talked about these things, and tried to make peace with Sharon in his own head.

Four years ago, when Sweets had been going through his second divorce, he began calling his estranged wife at her parents' house in

Chester, New Hampshire. He would wake her at midnight, one in the morning, two in the morning, and tell her he was learning how to forget her, tell her he loved her, tell her that she was a liar and a bitch. He made up stories about other women, told her their mutual friends saw his side of things, found corners of his heart he had never seen before. She listened quietly, waited out the storm of anger, and said, "You better not come up here. My father is here. My brother is here." There was a tremble in her voice, and he imagined her family rising from their beds and walking into her room—the room she had slept in as a child—to see what was the matter again. "They'll set you straight," she said, and it was like she had put the thought in his mind, like she had *wanted* him to come—an invitation, although of course it was anything but. He tried not to think about that.

"Let me see your hand," Sharon said.

"It's fine," he said, but he held it out to her, palm up, like he was begging. She touched it tenderly—it was almost like she knew what she was doing—and Sweets let her. He turned his hand over and moved his fingers, first one and then the next, until she was satisfied.

She said, "There are scars all over the back of your hand. I never noticed them before," and he thought of when he had broken the window, twisted the doorknob from the inside. He had just stepped into the house when her brother and father had appeared, and he had almost been glad to see them. He was almost glad to see their anger—how long had they been holding it in, maybe they were glad to see him too—and glad, definitely glad, not to see the disappointment in his wife's face. She was still his wife then.

He had been wearing the coat, and torn it on glass as he pulled his hand free. Then he was falling backward, and then standing and running, running and then walking to his truck, trying hard to get some pride back in those twenty feet from the back porch. He drove away with the headlights off, churning up dirt and gravel and not knowing how he had even come to be here, come to be *this* person. He pushed down on the gas and jerked the truck into third and thought, *This is what she'll remember.* That was not that long ago, not really.

He was forty-four years old and he figured he had fifteen good years left. Tomorrow they would lift the pig—the largest one, the one that had not made a sound—and set it over the barrel fire and then, when they were warm, he would put his hand on her knee and ask her something—he didn't have the words yet.

They would stuff themselves silly, and drink other people's beer, and watch the cinders spark up and swirl when they threw new logs on the fire. This night would become a wall between what had been and what would be, but right then, in the truck, he had to ask her something else. He said, "You think you'll ever forgive that guy for what he did to you?"

"Oh, Sweets," she said. "You're a good man, aren't you?" and she laughed, like there was a joke there somewhere. She shoved the stick into first and pulled into the road without checking for traffic.

Sweets said, "Hey, be careful," but he was too tired to raise his voice, and anyway, it was all clear.

THE CASTLE ON THE HILL

THEY HAD BEEN PLAYING WITH STICKS—sword fighting, thrusting, dodging, and hacking. Barry remembered that much, and the way they both parted as he drove down the road, one boy to the left of his truck, one to the right, giving him just enough room to pass. Then they held their sticks above their heads in mock salute, their faces red from cold and oh-so serious.

He had glanced up in his rearview mirror and watched them come together again in the middle of the road as he drove past, as if they owned it and he was just a nuisance.

This was nothing new. Kids didn't like the sight of the animal patrol truck. They probably thought he was up to no good, but he had no intention of stopping to pick up a stray even if he saw one. He deserved a break from time to time and so did the dogs.

He remembered thinking the same about the kids as they stepped aside to let him pass—that they were up to no good. What had they been doing up on the hill that early in the morning?

He took this route to work every day, partially because he liked the woods, partially because the other route would have taken him by his old house. He slowed the truck and watched the kids smacking their sticks together. Then they turned, looked at him, and ducked into the woods. They were probably headed up to the castle ruins. He was alone again. He sped up and headed down the hill to work.

Yes, he had thought as he watched them pull the branches back to make a path, *up to no good.* Only later, when he got the phone call from Kevin, would he think about them as what they were—children, not kids, but children. When Kevin told him what happened to them he would remember their serious faces and think, *If they had been smiling I would have stopped and offered them a ride.*

What else did he remember? That their coats were unbuttoned even though it was the coldest day of the year. That was not enough. He should have remembered more about the color of their clothes and the hats on their heads and whether or not their expressions were truly serious or just some invention of his memory. It seemed that he had been careless. He realized that as soon as Kevin told him what had happened.

"Did you see what's on the TV?" Kevin asked when he picked up the phone. It was the second call of a boring day, although that had been two more calls than he had expected.

"I've been at work since this morning," Barry said.

"Well, two kids were murdered out by the castle. They found the bodies earlier today, in the woods. They're not releasing the names."

Barry suddenly thought of his own two children, and he felt an instinctual shock of fear for their safety, but of course they were grown now, and what he felt was nothing but false shock—the kind of jolt that moves through you when a dog jumps and snarls and your body forgets about the sturdy chain around its neck. Then he thought of the children who had actually died—their wind-blown pink, intense faces—and felt ashamed that he had not thought of them first. He had seen them just that morning, after all. "Thanks for the cheery news, Kevin," he said. "You can fill me in on the details

14

tomorrow." Which meant, Let's just have a day where none of these things happen, at least in our minds, if nothing else.

"Sorry," Kevin said, and then, to U-turn the subject matter toward a place with a nicer view of the world, "I'm in my living room right now looking out at the snow. Nobody's here yet, but the smell from the kitchen is making me salivate, I swear to God."

"You paint a nice picture."

But Barry didn't imagine Kevin's house. He imagined his younger daughter Jamie's house with her safe inside, although she was probably at Sheila's. The turkey would probably be coming out of the oven right about now, and the kitchen would be warm. People would be eating snacks in the dining room, talking about innocuous subjects.

After he had hung up the phone he headed to the window and looked outside at the falling snow. He stood there listening to the wind scuttle across the tin roof, and then he lit a cigarette and smoked it and tried not to think about the castle or the children, who he imagined as still walking up there, still holding their thin, useless weapons. Stakes taken from a building site, he realized now, remembering how they had held them aloft. One end had been pointed, the other end painted bright orange. They hadn't been wearing gloves. He remembered that now—their bare fingers around the sticks, one palm open and raised but not waving. They must have been cold. For that reason alone he should have given them a ride.

He smoked the cigarette down and rubbed it out in the ashtray on the desk. It was the second of two he allowed himself each day, and as he ground it out, he felt sorry that he hadn't postponed the small pleasure until later that night.

The storm meant some extra cash because he was going to go

out plowing—that's what Kevin had really called to tell him, that he had the go-ahead to plow—but he wasn't about to be placated by a pretty scene or the chance of a paycheck. It was snowing, it was cold, and he was hungry. He really wished he hadn't wasted that stupid cigarette.

The first phone call that day had been from an old lady out on Essex Road by the old stadium. She had called the day before too, complaining about the dog in the apartment above hers. "They can't control their children, let alone an animal," she had said. She told him she could hear the barking in the early morning when she was still in bed, when the whole world was still in bed.

Let her wait, he decided, let Kevin wait. Let the roads wait. Let the whole city wait. He reached for the coal shovel against the wall. He had to stop soon, anyway, because he had left his gloves on the pantry counter right next to the cheese sandwich he had wrapped in tinfoil that morning.

After a few minutes of scraping the coal shovel across the tar he stopped and looked back at what he had accomplished. Not much, really, and he was already breathing hard. Of course, he had told himself he would *not* come to the pound, not today, but he found it difficult to stay at the apartment lately. He zipped his coat up to his neck and hunched back into his work. He knew what Sheila would say if she were here. She would have told him that he liked to complain, that he nursed his anger like a baby at a bottle.

Over the years, he had grown adept at seeing himself through Sheila's eyes. He wondered if that was a kind of love, and decided that yes, maybe it was. It was like being gifted with another sense, although often that sense was much too acute.

How did she see him anyway? Her husband of twenty-one years,

16

although not for the last two. A man who had not changed much in the time they had spent together, and would probably not change much in the future. Forty-six years old, the last dozen spent as an animal control officer. A fixture of the town, although not of her life.

He should not have answered the phone. He shouldn't have even come out here at all today—should not have taken the shortcut up and over the hill at the very least—but he had, and so the rest of the afternoon had been pushed into an awkward stumbling motion by those misguided little decisions. He headed to the truck and climbed inside. The snow was falling harder now. The spot he had shoveled had already turned white. It had been eight or nine years since it had snowed like this in November.

He turned the key, listened to the engine gasp, let it fall silent, counted to ten, then hoped for a small dose of luck as he turned the key again. The truck finally sputtered to life and he revved the engine a few times to keep it going. Then he lowered the plow and drove out past the recycling center, past the dumpsters and the cluster of maple trees where the police liked to hide, where he took a left onto Primrose Street. He imagined the two boys wandering into town toward home like travelers from far away, although of course they were not from very far away at all, and they weren't going home, and it seemed wrong somehow to think about them too much. After all, he had not even known them.

It was almost seven by the dashboard clock, which meant it was really six. The roads were just about empty. He liked being alone in this way—this was not loneliness, not like at the pound—because he was moving now, and there was the promise of company with no strings attached—that other car coming at you out of the dark, another person just as crazy as you for driving on a night like this.

Everybody who had been born in town knew it by its Indian name, Winnekenni, but most people just called it the castle. It had been built at the turn of the century by a rich Englishman whose name adorned a plaque on one of its fire-blackened walls. The man had built it for his wife, who was homesick for Britain, but supposedly it hadn't soothed her enough to make her stay very long. At least that's what people said, although there was another version of the story in which the man was American and only the woman was British, and in that story they had simply moved to California. In both stories, though, it was the woman who had named the castle, stealing an Algonquin Indian term meaning *very beautiful*.

After the couple had left town, the castle had changed hands regularly until it had burned down in the late fifties. Nothing but the stone shell had remained, but it had been sold and quickly rebuilt as a residence for a Boston lawyer. Then it had burned again in the late sixties. The lawyer had headed to New York, and it had sat unoccupied ever since, except for homeless people and vandals who peeled back the boards on the doorway and climbed inside. They spread blankets on the ground on cold nights and slept in huddled groups. They smashed bottles against its stone walls and played music on portable radios until the police came to investigate. And although most people would have considered them vandals, Barry felt these people had a right to the place by default, and that it was better off in the hands of drifters and drunks than a rich woman pining for the architecture of her childhood.

He could see it now, faintly, up on the hill that overlooked the town, not the castle itself but a shimmering kind of light, as if another fire was just beginning to take root in one of its inner rooms. It looked comforting and almost magical, and he wondered if the two kids had looked up at the same sight this morning from their vantage point in the woods, and if it had calmed them in the way it did to him now, and given them a false sense of hope.

He turned onto South Broadway and headed down into town, driving just a little faster than he should. The castle changed position, off to his left now. You could see it from everywhere, from downtown, out at the reservoir and the dump, from the new condos out to the east, from his new apartment. From Sheila's house, his old house.

He didn't talk to her much these days, but when he did she was always giving him second-hand advice, passed on from her friends, her yoga instructor, or her new husband. The new husband worked for a company that bought smaller companies, taking hold of them firmly and then picking them apart the way a hawk might dismantle a field mouse. "Change is good," was one of his mottoes.

You are defined by your actions, the yoga instructor said, or rather Sheila said, acting as mouthpiece for the instructor. "People are their actions," she told Barry once. "They're the same thing."

She had said this in the early days of the separation and it was supposed to function as a beacon to guide him through the approaching darker times. He was thankful for it—he was thankful for anything from her—although he had to wonder if that was all there was to a person. Because if everyone was simply the accumulation of what they had done in the world, well, he hoped people were more than that, hoped *he* was more than that. Was it fair to judge a person that way? What about the complexity of his intentions, the mystery of it all?

He was putting down more dogs the last couple of years. Things had grown worse since the other animal shelter opened just over the

border in New Hampshire. The red barn, the horses and the goats—
it was a nice picture, and when someone from this part of Massachusetts thought about adopting a pet, that's the picture they wanted
to make themselves a part of, not a small boxlike building hidden at
the edge of a dirt parking lot behind the recycling center.

He wondered how many animals they put down every day up
there. How many did he put down? He had a rough count in his
head, and he could take this number and multiply it by seven, and
then by fifty-two, and then by fifteen, but you know, what was the
point?

The woman came to the door on the third knock and Barry was
immediately sorry he had come here. From the awkward way she
leaned against the doorframe he could tell that she had been drinking,
and when she opened her mouth and said, "What's the matter, officer?"
the soft slur in her voice confirmed it. He disliked it when they confused
him with the police. In Lowell, two years ago, a Cambodian street gang
shot up a dog officer because they thought he was a cop.

"I'm from animal control," he said, as if he was just one small part
of some great governmental mechanism, and he let the realization
pass across her face. Over her shoulder he could see a man sitting at
the kitchen table, some dirty plates, a teenaged girl standing in the
doorway of what must have been her bedroom. There was a half-
dismantled turkey at the center of the table and the man was poking
at it with his fork, toying with it, the way people did when they were
stuffed but hoping for a second wind.

"There's been a complaint about your dog," he said.

The woman looked back at him with a befuddled you-have-the-

20

wrong-apartment expression. Then she turned, as if she had suddenly remembered something, and yelled, "Karen, the dog!" The teenaged girl walked over and took her mother's place—presumably it was her mother—wedged in the small space between the barely-opened door and the wall.

"There's been a complaint about your dog," he repeated.

"I'm sorry," she said. "I'm really sorry." The woman had taken a seat across from the man and they were both watching the girl's back as she spoke.

"Where is the dog?" he asked.

"In my bedroom. My boyfriend gave it to me a couple of months ago. On my birthday." This as a way to absolve herself of any guilt, he guessed.

She excused herself and returned with the dog, holding it by the collar as it tugged her across the kitchen. Some kind of Labrador mutt with maybe a little Collie thrown in, judging from its narrow face. It hadn't yet grown into its paws. "I can't really take care of it very well," she said.

"Yeah," he said. "It looks like a handful," and he immediately knew what she wanted. She wanted him to take the dog off her hands. He ruffled the fur at the back of its neck. He was ready to leave, to tell her to keep the noise down and close the door on his way out, but she had more to say.

"He's kind of a farm dog, you know?" she said. "He needs lots of open land. A family with land and maybe some kids." She said this in the usual hopeful way. She wanted him to pick up on the story she was telling herself, acknowledge its truth and its wisdom and then take the dog by the collar and lead it away. Or at least not tell her what she probably already knew: that a year-old mutt his size did not have much chance of being adopted, especially by some mythological farmer and his happy family.

He had often participated in this kind of exchange. I'll give you my dog and you give me a reassuring little story. But that wasn't the story he wanted to tell her. He knelt and felt around the dog's paws. Its nails hadn't been cut in a long time. They were splintered a bit, as if it had been scratching at some hard surface. He gave the dog a light pat on the rump and attached a leash to its collar. It circled half around him and then moved to the door. It was going for a walk.

He didn't understand, either, the skewed logic that determined which dogs were adopted and which were not. This is really what made him dislike the people who occasionally came by to gawk and poke and finally select whatever pet they thought was the right choice. He had decided long ago that they were *complicit* somehow, in a way they chose to ignore, in pretty much the way this girl was now. Although the crime was difficult to pin down, and if they *were* guilty then he probably was as well, and he had been told that one of his flaws was taking everything too seriously anyway.

When he got outside he walked the dog up half a block and back, letting it enjoy its illusion of freedom. It lifted its leg and marked a mailbox. He always asked for the dog's name, but this time he hadn't. The dog wasn't licensed either, which meant its name had pretty much ceased to exist when they had left the apartment. It would spend the next seventy-two hours without one.

He checked its ears, which were filthy, and then raised his hand above its head. The dog flinched and backed away. Someone had knocked it around a little. "Come here," he said, but the dog wouldn't jump into the truck cab. It seemed distracted by everything and anything: the rear bumper, a skeletal bush encircled with wire fencing, a sewer grate. Finally, he dug out a tennis ball from beneath the passenger's seat and threw it in the back.

That did the trick. The dog jumped after it without a second's hesitation. He slammed the door, almost disappointed that such a simple ploy had worked.

The truck started on the first try—no rhyme or reason there, of course—and as he pulled out into the road he suddenly realized where he was going next. Not back to his apartment, not back to work, or around and around the roads of the city like some wandering beggar. He was going to go to Sheila's house. He had been heading there all along, he realized, without knowing it. God, he was hungry.

"Marriages go bad all the time," she had said, but just because his was a story that was told over and over again didn't make it less important. Hell, it made it more important, didn't it? When people watched the six o'clock news and saw more murders and stabbings and beatings, they told themselves, oh yeah, that again, as if the more it happened, the less tragic it became. But they should have been up in arms. They should have been crying into their hands.

It would not have been that difficult to see all the dogs as one dog, the same dog dying over and over again. He knew he could do it if he wanted. But he simply didn't want to turn off that part of himself. It would have been easy to see his marriage as all marriages too, as the latest in a long, inevitable line, and himself as every man who had too quick a temper, too little compassion, but that would have been too simple, too comfortable.

Maybe this was how Sheila saw him: as someone who held on tenaciously to things past the point of reason.

23

There were seven cars at Sheila's house—at his house—parked in the driveway and trailing down one side of the street in tight line. Barry spotted her red Toyota and her sister's blue Mazda. He pulled up on the curb across the street, killed the engine, and watched the occasional silhouette in the window. He thought about lighting a cigarette but told himself that no, he could wait without one. In a way, he blamed Sheila for the embarrassment that he knew was coming. Why hadn't she simply moved to some other town? Her new husband certainly made enough money, right?

Maybe this guy was one of those blowhards who wore expensive suits and drove expensive cars but had maxed-out credit cards and a condo that had depreciated in value every year since he had bought it. For those kinds of people money wasn't something you held in your hand. It was as vague as air. It floated around them and they breathed it in and out without thinking. Barry liked to think of him that way. It made him more of a villain and Barry less of one.

Finally, someone appeared at the door, a couple deciding to brave the roads, dressed in the requisite holiday gear—long coats, sweaters, gloves. The woman leaned on the man as they almost tip-toed down the steps, him half a step ahead. There was a promise of thrills in what they were doing, as in most foolish decisions, and Barry wondered how hard the people inside had argued with them to stay. Without knowing why, Barry got out of his truck and headed over, intercepting them as the man was opening the passenger's side door.

"Barry?" the man said.

"Hey," Barry said, and they shook hands. It was one of Sheila's cousins from Maine. Jason or Bobby. How ridiculous to be standing in the cold shaking the hand of a person he hardly even knew. "It looks

24

like you've been having a good time," Barry said. "How's the party going?"

"It's going great," the man said, with a quick glance at the woman. She was halfway in the car. He walked quickly to catch up to her.

He felt them watching as he pushed the bell. What had Sheila told them about him? Everything? He remembered the argument in the front hall, the hall just on the other side of this door. It had been one of many, but it was the one he thought of now—him telling her he hated her in a quiet voice, and her stepping backward, back deeper into the house, expecting him to follow. His hand becoming a fist, and then uncurling again, as if letting something go. She had said that he should get out, repeating the words twice, once as a request, the second time as a command, although neither had seemed like the right way to ask.

"Who are you?" the little girl who answered the door said. It was a good question. He stepped inside and stomped his feet amidst the pairs of shoes and boots. He took off his hat and coat and threw them on a chair, then glanced at the dining room table, which was littered with dirty dishes and the bones of another dismantled turkey, larger than the one he had left behind. He recognized the pattern on the dishes. He had smashed one of those against the wall and she had bent down and begun to pick up the pieces. The sight of her kneeling there, undoing what he had done, had so angered him that he had thrown a second dish and a third and a fourth, but now here they were, a complete set again, the delicate loop of red and gold around the outer edge.

"My name's Barry," he said, and he held out his hand for the girl to shake. From the kitchen he could hear people talking and laughing, what he thought might be Sheila's voice telling a joke.

"You're late, you know," she said, but the girl took his hand and then released it.

"That's not true," he said, walking past her to the table. "I'm not even supposed to be here." He stabbed some turkey with a fork and looked around for an empty plate. The girl sat down next to him.

"Ever heard of a microwave?" she said, but she passed him the plate when his eyes fell there, and then the mashed potatoes, and then the stuffing. He was just spooning out the cranberry sauce when Sheila came in and rested her hands on the girl's shoulders.

"Vicki, could you do me a favor and go in the kitchen for a sec?"

He set his plate down—it was now piled with food—and the girl picked a piece of turkey off of it and chewed it slowly. Then she lifted the plate and carried it with her into the other room, as if Barry had given it to her.

"Hello, Sheila," he said, without looking at her, when the girl had gone.

"Barry," she said, with a small laugh. "This is a new low."

"I was in the neighborhood," he said. "I thought you'd want your driveway plowed."

"I'd like you to leave," she said, in a way that sounded more disappointed than angry.

He straightened up and took a deep breath. "Sure," he said. "I'm sorry. You're right." And he nodded his head, stood, and grabbed his coat. He was surprised, though, when she walked him to the front door, more surprised when she stepped outside with him.

"Who's the little wise-ass?" he asked, tilting his head to the door.

"Vicki," she said.

"No, I mean who does she belong to."

"Oh. Jenny and Bill. She's Jenny and Bill's kid. You wouldn't know them. Friends of friends."

He laughed at that without knowing why. "Friends of friends."

"That's right."

They looked out at the road. The windshield of the truck was already dusted with new snow. "Is Jamie in there?" he asked, knowing that she was not. She was in Gloucester with her husband's family, and Tammy, she was in Chicago, pregnant with a girl of her own. He was struck by the equality of this, that he and Sheila were both losing them in just about equal measure, in that slow, non-dramatic way many parents lose their children.

"No," she said. "She was thinking about it this year. But she decided to stay put."

"Yeah," he said.

"Let me ask you," she said. "What have you been doing lately?"

Something else to laugh at. "What have I been doing?"

"Yeah. What have you been doing?"

"I don't know. The usual."

"I do worry about you, you know."

"I know. But I'm fine." And as he said this he realized why he had come—to warn her. But he didn't know about what exactly—possibly the simple fact that there was danger in the world. The force of that truth struck him then, and he wanted to reach out and wrap his arm around her shoulder and lead her back into the house as if it were still his own. "Did you hear about those two kids?" he asked.

"No," she said, and he told her, although he didn't know much about it himself. "Oh, that's horrible," she said, when he was finished, and he could tell that she was thinking many things. Maybe she was thinking that she didn't know why she had come out here into the cold, to be with this man she had been married to once upon a time. He looked out into the weather at the dim outline of the castle in the distance. She would end up telling this story too, sometime after she

27

went inside, passing it along to the people who were just now getting curious as to where she had wandered off. "I should go," she said.

"Do you have to?" he asked.

"Of course I have to." Her voice was a little frayed now, but there was something tender there too. At least he thought there might have been.

"Okay," he said. "Okay."

"Well," she said. "Good. Take care of yourself."

"I didn't mean it," he blurted out, although he wasn't thinking of a particular incident. He hadn't meant a lot of things—he certainly hadn't meant to become this man standing in front of her today, speaking these words. "I didn't mean any of it," he repeated. "You know that, don't you? It wasn't really me."

That made her laugh a little. "Then who was it, Barry? If not you then who was it?"

How could he answer something like that? He touched her shoulder then, but she pulled away. He was instantly sorry he had done it. He had no right to touch her. "Please," he said. He felt that if he could just have ten minutes of her time, five minutes of her time, he could convince her. Convince her of what, exactly, he wasn't sure. Maybe that, yes, there was danger in the world—terrible, horrible danger—but not from him. He gritted his teeth and began to feel the old anger swelling up inside his chest. "Oh, Jesus," he said, and he began to laugh. Where the hell was that new husband of hers? Why didn't he do the chivalrous thing and come out here? Was he afraid of getting cold? Barry wanted to hurt him then, him and all the people who were watching them carry out their little performance. He could see their faces in the window. Was it too much to ask to let him come in for a little while and have a little something to eat? Was it too much for Sheila to forgive him for what he had done, even just for a night, an hour? Maybe that's why he had come here—to warn her, yes, but also to be forgiven, because what was what he had done compared to what had happened today up on that hill? But maybe nobody could forgive him, not even her, who had lived it with him.

When he looked into her eyes he could tell from the steadiness in her stare that it was over. Their marriage had been gone for a while now—he knew that—but something else was finished. "Well, happy Thanksgiving," he said.

"Yeah," she said.

People were still watching from the house as he turned the key and pumped the gas and cursed the damned city for not getting him a new vehicle last year. When the truck finally started, he climbed out and wiped away the snow from the windshield with his arm. And as he cleared the snow away, the door to her house opened again, and the little girl—Vicki, that was her name, right? She appeared holding something in her hands.

It was his hat. She ran down the steps as if it were summer, slid her feet along the walk, and looked both ways before crossing the street. "Hey," she said. "You forgot this."

"Oh," he said. "Oh, thanks."

She handed it to him. It was a wool cap he had owned forever, the kind of cap you could find in any store, but he would have missed it. He took it from her and smiled. "That's nice of you," he said, and he slid it down over his head.

"No problem," she said, and then, "What kind of dog is that?" The dog was looking at them from the truck, front paws up against the window. "It's a mutt, huh?" she said, before he could answer. Then another question. "What's his name?"

29

"Oh, he doesn't have a name," he said.

She looked suspiciously at him, as if he were trying to pull something on her. Something occurred to him then. He said, "You know, if you want to name it, go ahead."

"Really?"

"Sure."

She looked at the dog again. "It's hard to think of just one." She made her face into a sneer and he imagined the swirl of a thousand names that must have been going through her head.

He let the dog out of the truck and held it by the collar as it nuzzled up against her, desperate for any kind of attention. "He likes you," he said. He looked back over at the house and said, "You know, if you want him, you can have him. I'm just bringing him back to the pound."

She gripped his collar and said, "Really?"

"Sure."

He imagined the dog entering the house and the perplexed expressions of the people there. They would make small adjustments for it. They would feed it food from the table. It would find a warm corner and someone would take it home in their car at the end of the evening, maybe Vicki's parents, maybe someone else, but someone. It was a holiday, after all, and the girl seemed strong-willed, and who could resist a story like that?

This seemed like a small victory for his imagination. He said good-bye to the girl and drove away alone.

There were always more. A lean black shadow scrambled along in the breakdown lane of Lawrence Street, head lowered. It was a German Shepherd, big and angry looking. He drove past, U-turned, and stopped. It stopped too. They looked at each other. "Oh, great," he said, and he bent down and held out his hand. "Come here. Come here, girl."

When he got back to the pound Barry tried to walk the dog inside, but it whined and pulled so much he had to carry it in his arms to the building. He could feel the ribs where his hand rested against its side.

He returned to the truck for the food. There had been a sub shop open in town, a small Greek man in an apron playing an ancient video game. When he had seen the sign still lit up he had decided that it was a small miracle—fate giving him just what he wanted. But they didn't really talk about what they could have talked about—two men out on a night like this, with nothing better to do. The man's English was not good, just good enough to take the order. Two steak and cheese subs and a diet soda.

So he brought the subs inside and took off his coat and threw it over a chair. The dog was staring warily at him from across the room. "I don't blame you," he told it, and he leaned forward and set a piece of the steak on the ground. The dog nudged forward and lapped it up, swallowed it whole, leaving a small smear of grease and spittle on the ground. Barry set the second piece there, and the third piece, a little closer. The fourth, he held out in his hand. The dog took that piece from his palm gently, lapping at his fingers, and the next one, and the one after that. "There you go," he said, and when the dog was finished—when it was curled up in the corner and almost asleep—only then did he allow himself to eat.

SHOW & TELL

The Decapitated Android

Someone has twisted off its head.

This had once been a pretty great toy, but now only a small rubber stem extends from its stump of a neck. If a head were placed there—the correct head—and screwed into position, the thing would be just like new. The joints at the elbows and knees are still strong, the cool-ass silver paint unscratched, and a small switch in its back, when pressed, reveals not one, not two, but a row of three machine guns hidden in a panel in its beefed-up, no-nippled chest.

That first time Heineken brings you into the walk-in closet, this is the toy you see, this is the toy you have to have, because even though it's broken, ninety percent of it is *the fucking neatest thing you've ever seen*. You reach for it, hold it in your hand, imagine that the head is around there somewhere, in one of those old boxes, and that you're going to find it and make it whole and when it's healed you're going to stuff it under your shirt and tell him you have to get going. You've never stolen anything bigger than a pack of gum in your life, but your animal instincts kick in, and you want it with a greed that surprises you. It's just that slick.

Heineken pushes shirts out of the way so he can climb to the back of the room. It's more like a room than a closet, you realize, as the shirts part and you can see the length of it. It has a small window at

33

the far end that looks out onto their large yard. He looks out the window, then turns and slides down into a crouching position. "This is where she put all his stuff," he says.

His nickname is Heineken because he once drank one of his dad's Heineken beers out behind the school, in broad daylight, during school hours, or least this is the story he told you when you met at the beginning of the summer, at the scrub-brush baseball diamond at the end of your block. He was wearing the same shirt then that he is today—a yellow T-shirt with "Star Wars" written across it in space-aged block lettering. You often lie awake at night wondering why you're the only person in North America who hasn't seen this movie. But you're not about to beg your brother to drive you, so you say you've seen it four times, one less than Heineken, who repeats the storyline enough that you feel like you really *have* seen it.

"If she knew we were fucking around in here she would go ape shit," he says, as he wipes the back of his arm across his nose.

When you grabbed Kool-Aid from his fridge just an hour ago, you noticed that there were Heinekens there in the vegetable crisper, four of them placed end to end in rows of two, like batteries. "Yeah," you say, even though you have never seen his mother, know nothing about her temper or why this place is off limits. That comes later.

"It's hot in here," he says. "I'm sweating like a pig."

You make a sound like your brother sometimes makes, deep in the back of your throat, halfway between a burp and a snicker. It's a sign that you have better things to do, even though you don't. You have discovered another secret about the android. The machine guns are hollow and fire real projectiles, little slivers of plastic with red rubber ball ends. You find one on the shelf, slide it into the barrel, cock the switch in its back, and hear the click.

It is the kind of thing little kids swallow. They fire it into their open mouths. Then you read about them in the newspaper.

Cool.

Satan's House of Horror

The cover has been torn off but you know it's issue twelve because you've read the fine print. All the secrets of the comic are written in the box at the bottom of the first page in type so small it feels like a joke at your expense: the year it was printed, the address of the publisher, the subscription rate for the comic in the United States and Canada, and the words *No similarity between any of the names, characters, persons, and/or institutions in this magazine with those of any living or dead person or institution is intended, and any such similarity which may exist is purely coincidental.*

Above these words, a brightly colored splash page shows a devil peering down at hordes of people stewing in a gigantic vat of molten lava. The Satan-figure has raised its pitchfork, because maybe one of these people might try jumping out of the lava, to scramble away to safety, and it needs to be ready to spear that person through the heart. The rest of the comic has nothing to do with this image—when you leaf through the pages you find three boring ghost stories—but this one page rocks. The devil is smiling like crazy. You've never seen anybody so happy.

And then the creepy thought occurs to you, the so-scary-it-makes-you-proud idea. There are so many squirming bodies in that vat that some of them are probably *bound* to look like real people— statistically speaking—despite the tiny words proclaiming that any such similarity is purely coincidental.

"He had a shit load of comics," Heineken says. He's watching you as you read. Occasionally he asks if you want to catch some TV, go to the pond and throw rocks, have some nachos, but sprawling on his bed with a stack of his brother's comic books is ten times better.

"Where is Oregon?" you ask, because that's where Heineken has told you his brother moved when he was sixteen.

"It's on the other side of the country," he says. "It's practically Alaska."

Sixteen seems just old enough to make an ambitious move like that. You're eleven now and in five years you are going to be a completely different person—and not a person like your own brother, who at nineteen slides his feet across the pocked kitchen linoleum like a tired fifty-year-old. You hear him from your bed when he comes home from work, his feet sliding, his keys clicking on the glass tabletop in the kitchen. The door to the room you share opens and he clicks on the light, and then the TV, and you push your face into the darkness of your pillow.

Inside the comic book, a ghost in a black hood is walking down a corridor, dragging chains that create a long sound effect that spirals out of the panel and into the next one, where a man cringes in his bed, listening. This is stupid stuff you are reading, but you need to find out the end. You really hope somebody gets snuffed.

The ghost is passing through the door, arms extended, his hair like smoke trailing from the back of his head. The man is screaming, and something about their common expression—two mouths agape, two sets of eyes bulging, the similar caveman slope in their foreheads— makes it look like they are relatives in an especially ugly family.

You think that anybody could do bullshit like this; you could do it right now if you had a crayon and five minutes.

Stupid Rubber Werewolf

On Tuesday you play with marbles, holding them up to the light like jewels so you can see their shiny hypnotic centers. On Thursday you uncover a box of books—sword and sorcery paperbacks, thick science textbooks, a dog-eared collection of car photographs—and discover his name written neatly on the inside cover of each one. The next day you rummage through the pockets of a dungaree jacket and produce four things: a petrified stick of gum, a quarter, a ticket stub to a Black Sabbath concert, and a small werewolf made from rubber and wire. You bend its hands above its head, its legs into painful-looking pretzel-shapes. Of the three big Hollywood monsters—Frankenstein, Dracula, and the Wolfman—the Wolfman is potentially the coolest, but this guy you're twisting around is not very cool at all, and you have no idea why someone would carry it around in a jacket as sleek and dirty-amazing as the one hanging from the wire hanger.

"Want to eat?" Heineken says.

"Sure," you say. Heineken's father works in Boston and his mother works in Lowell and they leave meals for him wrapped in cellophane when they leave for the day. He always offers half of them to you, but you never accept. Instead you open the cabinets, find something familiar—a can of tomato soup—and plop it in a pan.

Heineken watches as you click on a burner and shake the pan above the flame. Your mother waters soup to thinness, or yells at you if you overcook the eggs, so this is good, this is better than the eating itself, and at first you serve Heineken too—a bowl, a spoon, and then a piece of bread taken from the fridge. But he says no, and looks at the soup like he's not sure where it came from. You want to tell him, *Look, this is yours*, but you eat separately—him his sandwich, you your soup—and you're rushing to finish because today is Friday and you're running out of closet-time. In a few hours you will walk home and you won't see Heineken until Monday, when once again he will appear at the boring little playground where you first saw him hanging limply from the jungle gym. Then you will head to his house together, Heineken walking slightly ahead, talking loud about what he did with his parents that weekend. This is how it works.

You've thought of showing up here some rainy Sunday morning and ringing the bell, but you remember another kid in another city, last year, and the way his head appeared in the upstairs window when you knocked on his door, and then that long wait, the second knock, the stupid shamble back down the stairs and out into the street, where you picked up a rock and thought of throwing it hard at the spot where the face had been just a few seconds before.

The first taste of the soup ignites your hunger, but you rest the spoon in the bowl and let your appetite stand. "What did William do?" you ask, trying out the name from the inside cover of the books. It does not feel that unnatural on your lips, especially with one of his quarters in your pocket and the werewolf on the table.

"Who?"

"William."

"Billy," Heineken corrects you.

Then he goes back to chewing like this is some kind of answer.

Giant-Sized Super Spectacular

There's at least one lesson to be learned from every object, and then something to learn when objects are put together in combinations of two or three, like the Matchbox car you found hidden inside a plastic submarine, but for the most part these lessons are beyond words. And the simplest lessons, the ones that appear in sentence form in your head, are as unsatisfying as your mom's mottos about *people making their own luck* and *respect being earned and not given* and sometimes, when she is especially tired, *tomorrow being a new day*. For instance: Super-villains are always trying to take over the world. Superheroes are always trying to stop them. That's the lesson in the comic book you are reading.

It seems like the millionth time these characters have fought, but there are no other issues before this one that help to explain what's happening. Why do The Lightning Dynamo and The Boomerang Kid dislike each other so much? The villain with the lizard skin keeps mentioning revenge, but revenge for what? It makes you think of September, that sick-stomach feeling that comes on you when you walk down the hall for the first time and everybody else is calling each other by name. You're this close to crumpling the stupid thing up, but you like the drawing, and one of the villains is sleek like a cat and has claws for hands.

"What does he do out there?" you ask. You are thinking that he maybe draws these things, comics like the one spread on the living room floor.

"Where?" Heineken asks. He's reading too. A Boy Scout manual.

"Oregon," you say. "Your brother."

"He's a boxer," Heineken says, and his eyes do this screwy thing they've never done before. They look up and off to the right, into the far corner where the ceiling meets the wall, and for a second you think he's heard a car in the driveway. You're ready to bolt down the stairs and out the back, into the thick woods behind their house. "A professional boxer," he says, limply, and your leg muscles relax.

You imagine him, sleek and shiny-wet, throwing punches at the air. It is like a scene from an old movie except there is no plot, no dialogue, just the empty ring, the one mysterious character, and the sandpaper shuffle of his feet.

"It's going to rain," you say, but you stay where you are, flipping the pages of the comic back and forth without really looking at them.

You walk home through a light drizzle that makes the blacktop of the road glisten. You take the long route past the train station, and when you finally arrive at your front door the little house is dark except for a light in your mother's bedroom. So you head in through the back door and make a peanut butter sandwich by the light of the open refrigerator. When you finish you close the door with your foot and eat the sandwich standing in the dark. Your mother calls something out and you answer with a mumbled hello as you chew. Then you wipe the crumbs off your hands above the sink and head into the bedroom. You could have sworn you put the headless android under your bed, but there it is leaning against the lamp on your nightstand, standing at attention like it's been waiting up for you. Its head stem spears a small note, which you grab and ball up, think about throwing on the underwear-littered floor. But you open it and find your brother's scribbled handwriting. *Are you going through people's trash now? Show some self respect. Love, Gerry.*

You'll have to hide the comic books somewhere better.

Broken Water Rockets

Two long rockets with hollow ends that can be filled with water from a plastic hand pump. A drawing on the box shows a rocket flying into the air and droplets of water exploding through the sky. Two smiling cartoon kids look up from the ground, waving their hands like they're saying good-bye.

You are getting too old for this.

You love it though. Your own toys—the bag of plastic solders, a machine gun that goes clack clack clack when you pull the trigger, even your plastic bat with duct tape wrapped around one end— they've all gone unused since you moved here in May, but Heineken's brother's toys are special. You want to keep digging. And anyway, the summer is a little secret between you and Heineken. In the fall things will be different. You know that. You're pretty sure he does too.

"Damn it," you say, when the rocket spurts up half a foot in the air and falls to the driveway blacktop. You pick it up again, begin pumping the stupid pump again, and then swear again when it still doesn't work. "Damn it to hell."

You've developed a habit of swearing like a sergeant in the war movies your brother watches late at night when he comes home from his new job at the 7-Eleven. It's his third this summer, and your mother is already talking about moving again. She says there are jobs in Florida, and the weather there is beautiful year-round. She has mentioned Washington state too, which you now know from a quick glance at a map is not that far from Oregon, but you're guessing it's a lot of baloney, like the time she wanted to go to Greece to check up on some old rich relative who probably doesn't exist.

"Your brother sure bought some stupid crap," you say, as you think about your own modest toys.

"Shut up," he says. He's not even looking at you. He's kicking at the grass near the two-car garage, trying to find June bugs. This yard is so different from the small square of dirt behind your own house. Sometimes you see a family of rabbits huddled around the back porch, or a single deer staring at you from the safety of the woods, and you watch them for as long as you can before they scramble away from you.

You are getting sick of the sight of Heineken's big flat face, his shirts with the little alligator on the chest, his pale little legs. You do some quick math in your head, trying to guess at how old he was when his brother left home, but you come up with nothing. The facts don't seem coherent yet. It's still like a bedtime story, something sleepy and faraway. "What was it you said before about the boxing?" you ask, and he shrugs his shoulders. He seems to do that more and more as you get to know him, although maybe you're just noticing it now. "You're a God damn liar," you tell him.

"Yeah, well, you're a God damn thief," he says.

You pick up the rockets and hold them while Heineken fills them with the hose.

The Other Robot

This one is not nearly as good as the headless android, but it's kind of fun to smash with the hammer you find in Heineken's cellar. It's lower jaw is larger than its upper jaw and as the hammer comes down on its chest, it seems to be frowning at you like the little Buddha your mother keeps on the dashboard of her Chevy Impala. When your brother drives, he talks to it like it's a passenger, asks it where it's headed, then answers with a high, I'm-so-funny voice. "Canada!" it says back. Or, "Arkansas!"

You imagine the hammer accidentally coming down on your thumb and turning it blue. You sort of hope it does; then you would have something to be mad at Heineken for, because it is his hammer. But your swings come down hard and precise, in the same spot every time, directly on the chest, which has fractured open to reveal a little clockwork mechanism.

"What are you doing?" Heineken asks from behind you.

"Fixing something," you say, without breaking the sharp upward swing, the downward slam. He turns and heads back into the living room, where he will probably sit in front of the TV and watch Donahue push a microphone into the faces of his studio audience members.

It doesn't feel like you're lying. There's something important inside, a little system of interlocking teeth and tiny rubber bands, and you want to see it as completely as you can. But as you break it open you are also smashing it flat. When you stop, Heineken comes back, but he doesn't say anything. "What?" you ask. You're breathing hard through your mouth.

"That was my brother's," he says.

"It wouldn't work," you say. "I was trying to fix it."

"He won that at the carnival," he says, "just before he left. We won it."

The word *the* before *carnival* pisses you off, like there is only one carnival in the entire world and you're supposed to know about it. "It's not like he's coming back for it," you say, but he's already walked away. You lift the hammer and bring it down a couple more times.

The landlord has been calling the house. You pick up the phone in the evening and he asks if your mother is there. You have orders to tell him she is in the shower, so this is what you tell him even though she's sitting at the kitchen table scanning the newspaper. She lifts her head and smiles.

"Go tell her it's me," he says, because he's called enough that he's stopped introducing himself.

"She's in the shower," you say.

"I know that," he says, so you hang up the phone. It begins to ring again. You walk away from it. So does your mother.

43

Rusted Scimitar

You know this word from some movie you saw just a few weeks before on Heineken's TV, so when you find one at the back of the closet behind some old clothes it's a doubly satisfying discovery. It makes you feel strong to slide your hands around the grip and lift it, smart to know its real name. What do people call this? Luck.

You are wearing a plastic army helmet you found at the bottom of a box and although the two items do not fit together at first, with a little imagination you can picture yourself as a time traveler who has picked up these odd items on all of his journeys through history. When you emerge from the closet, you feel so tough that you wave the scimitar around and say, "I could chop off someone's head with this."

You suddenly remember the decapitated android. Where did that thing end up, anyway? The last time you saw it was on your brother's pillow. He had pushed an orange down on its stem as a makeshift head, wrapped a napkin around its shoulders as a cape.

"Watch it," Heineken says. "That thing is sharp."

Which it is. You touch your thumb to it and draw a small droplet of blood, which you wipe on the front of your jeans.

You point the sword at his chest and say, "Was your brother a pirate? Is that what he was?"

"Cut the shit," he says.

You can hear the cars driving up and down the street outside. It's a little past five o'clock—the latest you've ever been here—and the chances of one of those cars being driven by Heineken's mother grows greater every second. You poke the sword forward, move it in the shape of an X. He rolls his eyes. He's bored of this, bored of you, and he wants you to be gone. All summer you've been thinking you're the one who chooses to leave before they get home, but no, you can tell now, he's been the one prodding you out the door. He's ashamed of your dirty Keds and your hungry belly.

"A pirate," you say, because somehow you know this hurts.

"Shut the fuck up about my brother," he says.

There is something tense and dangerous here but you want to keep prodding it to see if it bites back. You raise the sword to his face. It's close enough that you could lean forward and tap his nose with the point, but all he needs to do is step back two steps. You kind of wish he would.

"If he was here right now he would kick your ass," he says.

"A knight," you say. "Your knight in shining armor."

You are putting on your brother's I'm-too-funny Buddha voice and you hate yourself for it. You're almost relieved when Heineken slaps the sword to one side with the flat of his hand and throws a punch at your face. You duck your head and his hand hits the top of your head and then you are in there, grabbing him and pushing him back against the flower-print wallpaper. He grabs you too, in a grotesque little wrestling hold. You can hear him breathing hard. You can hear yourself too.

"Let me the fuck go," you say.

"You first."

Where is the scimitar? For a scary-fantastic second, you think you have accidentally impaled yourself, that blood is pouring down your back. You are not scared of dying or the hospital, but the idea of staining the wall-to-wall is almost too horrible to imagine, and if Heineken were not gripping you tightly, you would clutch your shirt and try to stop the warm flow. But the wetness on your back is just your own sweat. You fumble for a better position, slide your hands down his body. You can feel his ribs. "One, two, three," you say. "One, two, three," and you both let go at the same time, step backward, stare each other down. Your shirt is torn down the front in two places. The scimitar is on the floor. You hear the front door opening, or think you hear it, so you run downstairs and out the back like a thief, where Heineken's mother is standing, her car keys still in her hand. "Hello," she says, like she had expected you.

You don't say a word.

"Where did you get that hat?" she says.

"It's a helmet," you say, like a moron.

She reaches out and plucks it off your head and for a second, you think she's going to put it on her own head, but she holds it with two hands against her belly. You remember a funeral in one of the war movies, with a flag draped casket and a captain, the star of the movie, holding his cap that way. She says, "Are you a friend of Bobby's?"

It's like you're trying very, very hard not to exist.

"You were playing in the closet," she says.

"Why do you keep all those things?" you ask.

The moment hiccups as you wait for her to push her face into the correct expression—flat and stern and unemotional. "You're not supposed to be in there," she says, and although she isn't moving, you duck and scamper to your right, running past her and into the woods. When you are far enough away you stop and cup both hands to your mouth. You struggle to think of something to say, anything, and finally you yell out, "He's dead! He's dead!" but not loud enough for anyone to hear but you.

It's like a game you used to play sometimes. A half-dozen kids wandering through the woods holding plastic water pistols and machine guns that made clicking sounds when you pulled the trigger. You'd shoot someone and then yell something guttural at him

46

when he didn't fall down. He would shoot back and yell too, and pretty soon you'd be arguing about who had been hit, who had missed. Remembering this, you yell out a little louder, "He's dead!"

Your voice sounds strange—distant, as if someone else is yelling those words at you, from off somewhere in the forest. You lower your hands, spin around and give the trees a once over, expecting to find Heineken there, holding the scimitar. Maybe smiling in a way you've never seen before—sinister and confident—or maybe wearing a face like his mother's when you asked the question about the closet. But of course he is not. Not even a squirrel or rabbit to act as an excuse for that scaredy cat feeling of being watched.

You pick up a good, straight stick and point it at an invisible enemy, mumble the words like a little curse.

Home-Made Android Head

It's not really. It's just a ball of black duct tape pushed down on the stem. You slip an old action hero helmet over it and it looks pretty good, good enough that you think of giving it to Heineken as a gift. But your brother finds it first and he tells you that you're pretty resourceful for a retard and that he's going to donate it to the retard museum. He holds it above his head, tempting you to make a grab for it, but you just chew on your lip until he takes it away.

You guess that this is the last time you'll see it, and you guess right. Years later, when talking to him on the phone, you'll sometimes wonder what he did with it, if he dropped it in the trash or gave it away or left it someplace you really should have looked if you had just been smarter. But it's not all bad luck that day, is it? Because your mother comes home red-faced and smiling. She hugs you before she even closes the door and says that she just won the lottery. For a split-

47

second you imagine one million, two million, three million dollars—your mind spins you out of the house and across town and into some brand new life—but it's five hundred bucks, which is still a lot of money, and you hug her back.

She has lobsters in the car, she says, and you help her bring them inside. Their claws, you notice, are held shut by thick rubber bands. There are three of them, one for each of you in the family, and corn on the cob, and bottles of wine and beer, and strange little multicolored cookies wrapped in green cellophane. There are more groceries in the trunk of the car than you've seen in your life, and you have to take five trips to get them all inside. When you're finished your mother pulls you into her arms again and tells you to close your eyes. But before you can she hands it over. It's a baseball glove—somehow she managed to smuggle it inside without you seeing—and she hands it over with a flourish and a small kiss.

She drinks a glass of wine and watches you flex your hand, pound your fist into the base of the glove, and hold your arm out like you're ready to receive a hard pitch. The glove's too big for you, but you make a show of loving it, and she even brings up little league, although by this time she's rambling about all sorts of ambitions and regrets and stupid men and signing you up for little league suddenly becomes one of a million things she should have done with her life.

"Christ," she says, with a little laugh, when she catches herself crying.

That night when she's asleep you lift the lid from the garbage can. You slide your fingers in, push aside coffee grounds and vegetable muck and sharp lobster shells, but it's not there.

You think of walking to Heineken's house in the dark, but even you are smart enough to know that it would be pointless. When your brother comes in—he was supposed to be home hours ago—you are still awake, lying in the dark. "Where is it?" you say, with as much venom as you can bring up from your gut.

"Where is what?" he says. You can hear him pulling off his heavy shoes, dropping them to the floor. You'd push it a little more, but you know he'll push back, and you had your revenge anyway, because after waiting for him for an hour at dinner, you and your mother split his lobster between you.

"Forget it," you say.

"Forget what?" he says, with a snicker.

You are thinking of Heineken's face, the stiff puppet expression, the point of the scimitar. His features had been as much a mystery as the objects in the closet and you wanted to poke it to see if it would grimace the way you grimaced when you raised that single drop of blood on your thumb. Not even a poke. A jab at the air and a flinch would have been enough. It would have been like a gift to you if he had just twisted his face to show a little pain. But he didn't do it, so why should you give him the repaired android with its ridiculous duct tape head? You'll have to be satisfied with this odd balance, this double withholding.

You don't know what he feels, though, or what he thinks.

You've never even been in his room.

You tell yourself you won't go back there.

Little Green Soldiers

"Where is he then?" you ask.

"Shut-up," says Heineken.

You're standing in his yard throwing tennis balls up onto the roof of his garage. They slide down and you catch them and throw them up again. Sometimes one gets stuck in the gutter, and you poke at it with a broom handle until it pops free.

This is what passes for fun now. You haven't been inside in a week, ever since you held the scimitar in your hands and wore his brother's helmet on your head.

"You don't know, do you?" you say.

"Shut-up," he says. "Shut-up."

The summer is ending and when school starts in two weeks you know you're going to switch allegiances and attach yourself to a group of bruisers, like you did at the last school in Pittsburgh. Spitting, kicking, knotty-muscled kids who live in houses like your house. You are becoming one of these kids. Becoming isn't even the right word. You are one. And after that? In twenty years you will become *me*, and I will look for you over my shoulder as you scramble along the confused landscape of my history. In a way, you are as mysterious as that small space at the end of the hall, the missing brother. I am trying to rebuild you from scraps—smudged memories, damaged imagination. I guess I am trying to talk to you.

So when you get home you take your own pitiful little army men—the man with the binoculars, the sharpshooter, the captain, and all the rest—and burn them with your brother's naked lady lighter. They move in slow motion as they melt. Their arms curl inward. Their knees buckle. Their heads bow in prayer, and then you bury them in unmarked graves along the wire fence at the back of the yard, stand up and brush the dirt from your jeans.

"It's too late in the year to do that," your mother says, when she comes up behind you and puts her hands on your shoulders. She thinks you're planting seeds.

POSTERITY

THE WATER BUBBLER GURGLES AND SPITS TO LIFE. It is the Senator's way to stop time. The small crowd hesitates, stretches a little further down the hall, elasticlike, before pulling back and gathering around him. He lets the water run until it is cold, then touches his lips to the stream, but only for a second. "Senator," his assistant says, "we should really be going."

"Yes," he says. "Yes. Of course."

"Senator," she says. Small fragments of crowd separate themselves and move ahead, a person here, a person there. "Senator, please."

"Yes. I know."

He straightens up. It's time for the slow walk to the elevator. He raises his hand toward the handful of bored-looking photographers—half as a wave, half to shield his eyes from the flashes—and then his assistant puts her hand at his back and they are walking, trailing the crowd behind them. "I'm hungry," he says, still smiling. It's hard not to smile, even though he is not feeling well. His face, it's too accustomed to public life.

His assistant says something he doesn't catch—placating, smooth, almost motherly, although she's a third his age if she's anything. As his feet move he scans the walls for a clock, a window. Is it day? Is it night? "Just some paperwork to look over," she says.

That one gets through. It has the tone of command to it.

51

He looks at her, the rigid pulled-back hair, the determined eyes, the wide African nose, and decides she is heartless. She is trying to kill him slowly. Revenge for 1964, 1957, 1948, back even further, his father on her mother, his grandfather on her great aunt, back to someone screaming an indecipherable language in some tree-choked place on the other side of the world. What would it feel like to make love to her?

It's imbecilic, he thinks, to make everything you say a matter of record. Time slides by and your words harden around you until you're stuck, for everyone to see. He tries to think of something to tell her that will make her feel better, that will make him feel better, but that look, the efficient stare, it drives the words from his head. Where is she taking him? Who hired her anyway?

"Turn, Senator."

He turns as the elevator doors open behind him. He teeters there for a second, unsure, before he opens his mouth and lets instinct take over. "Thank you all very much for your attention today. I've seen lots of friendly and familiar faces. Take care now. Take care." They are backing into the elevator: him, the assistant, and two others, tall sunglassed men with thin lines for mouths, making their getaway. There is a short burst of questions, like gunfire, before the doors close. He catches half the words, the usual applesauce about missed meetings, his ex-wife's tell-all book, and what about the coming election? He's not thinking of running now, is he?

He ponders the slight space between his nose and the doors. It's what's left when the faces blur and the questions repeat themselves: an awareness of distance. The footsteps it takes to get somewhere. The nameless person an inch from his ear. The swallowing height of the domed ceiling as someone enters the second hour of a filibuster.

As he gets older, as his body shrinks and bends, he's noticed signs of his amassing authority. The reporters keep back out of frightened politeness. The increasingly longer pauses in his conversation are heavy with importance. He pictures himself eight years from now, his age crossed over into the strange world of triple digits, an ever-widening circle of onlookers around him as he step-slides from limousine to the double glass doors of some St. Louis hotel. Each word a declaration, each joke swelled with wisdom.

He has seen many things go the way of the Dodo Bird: dime comic books, all-white lunch counters. But this, it's a strange feeling, to be on the verge of outliving the century that's encompassed you for so long. He is heading someplace new. He is going there alone.

As the elevator floors slide by he rubs his hand across his bald head meditatively, feeling the small baby-hairs, the chapped skin. "That went well," someone says. The girl again.

"Yes," he says. A good word. It gets him through.

"But possibly more directness next time. Definitely more directness, actually."

"Fine. Fine."

"Directness is key in avoiding certain connotations. Directness and volume. Volume walks hand-in-hand with directness."

"Of course."

"And enunciation. It's fine to have directness and volume but without enunciation we start picking up those connotations I've been mentioning. Think of it as a three-sided triangle." She laughs quietly, almost shyly, to herself. "Like there's any other kind, right?"

He is thinking about the places he shares a name with: a kidney-shaped lake, several streets, a room in the Capitol, a couple of ugly lawless schools. It's a game he plays with himself, a way to travel. He leaves his body and floats around a little. He is many places at once.

53

"Watch your step, Senator."

He is writing a book in his head, four, seven, sometimes nine books, shifting and separating and merging slowly, like tectonic plates. Thoughts on politics, baseball stadiums, pretty girls, bourbon. It will be deep, whatever it is—a long look down the dark well of history. It will crash into his ex-wife's thin account, force it down and under. A series of books. Basic books. For people without bookcases. A whisper in the ear of America.

He has a tendency toward self-aggrandizement. He's known this for a long time.

"Let's scrap the hand-in-hand metaphor," she says. "It's trite. And we're not about triteness. Except where it connects with tradition, which I suppose goes without saying. A certain amount of triteness allows for connections with pivotal sections of your constituency."

The doors open and they move from elevator to lobby to sidewalk to car, from air-conditioned metal box to air-conditioned metal box. They slide easily into traffic, merging with the general vehicular flow. They are moving up the on-ramp, driving along the interstate. The Senator's eyes are closed and he is swaying slightly from side to side, as if in response to a breeze, first to his assistant's shoulder, then to the tinted window, back and forth.

He is dimly aware of a small push, her shoulder against his, and his forehead comes to rest against the window, where he falls asleep. His dreams are full of flotsam and jetsam: trapped yellow jackets crawling up the neck of a Coke bottle; a balloon shrinking in his hands; his father nodding his head at the stairs, *Go to bed, go to bed*. He tries to speak in the dream, but his lips do not work. I'm asleep, he wants to say, I'm only asleep, that's all, and that's all this is really about.

The smooth highway motion eventually gives way to a familiar slow, circular movement, the pop and crunch of gravel beneath the tires. The Senator opens his eyes. They are parked at the end of the long cul-de-sac driveway. His assistant leans close. "Senator, you're home."

He walks down the side of the house, where he pauses and kicks at frozen snow to widen the path. His assistant is standing just behind him, holding a folder of papers: yellow, white, and pink. Patient as a mule. He thinks of getting a shovel, because he's ruining his shoes, or maybe heading out to the barn to check on the horses, but he decides against it. Too far. Too cold.

When was the last time he walked out there? He misses it, misses them, the two ponies especially, their brown muscle sheen, the smell of urine-soaked hay, and most of all the shape of the barn in the distance as he moved closer through the overgrown grass. Often the anticipation of a thing is better than the thing itself. He's learned that one often enough.

He tries to lose her around back by entering through the servant's entrance and cutting through the kitchen, but she's right behind, helping with the door.

At the center of the kitchen is a large wooden chopping table covered with cutlery and strands of garlic. He contemplates a jumble of just-washed cooking implements on the sideboard, objects he can't quite decipher a use for, clamps and squares and whisks. They look like torture devices from some less civilized age. The table is large enough to sleep on. So are some of the countertops. You could practically take a bath in the double sink. Ceilings he couldn't touch if he stood on a chair. Rooms honeycombing in all directions. A house to play hide-and-seek in. An organism unto itself. And the kitchen, this is the heart of it, the warm place deep inside where the bustling domestic flow pumps in and out.

And the heart of the kitchen, he decides, is the refrigerator, recessed in the wall, humming efficiently. The sight of it fills him with a vague uneasiness. The sheer spotless white mass of it, two shoulder lengths wide, big enough to fit a man in comfortably. Two men. Who needs a refrigerator so large? He does, he guesses, as he opens the door and hears the soft slide of rubber against rubber. It's full of clear plastic containers, lime-greens, tomato-reds, sauces and more sauces. Below them, in the transparent fruit drawer, oranges and apples and pears, so large and polished as to appear fake. Two pineapples. Eggplant. Something else, small and spiny and vaguely alien. On the door there are cartons of skim milk and eggs and margarine and a seemingly endless supply of exotic condiments.

He can't break the pristine order. He has the strange sense that something bad would happen if he did, if he so much as let his fingers come to rest on a cucumber. He lets the door go and walks away, down the hall toward his study, his assistant moving along with him, as if attached by an invisible cord. They pass a couple of cleaning people he doesn't recognize, a middle-aged woman rubbing circles in a window, a man walking purposefully in the other direction. Quick nods are exchanged. He feels as if he is intruding on something private and serene.

There is only one chair in the study, a recliner covered with duct-taped gashes, so the girl positions herself against a wall, almost statuelike, folder held against her chest. The Senator sits down, tucks a quilt around his legs, and listens to his heart slow.

The shelves are mostly bare, a dictionary, a few law periodicals, a dozen copies of his ex-wife's book for the fireplace. The rest of his library, he's given that away, a gesture they had been worried about, the people around him. Giving things away, that can be misconstrued, they had told him, holding up their hands in warning. Great, great potential for misunderstanding. But he was sick of all that paper, books he had never even touched, others he hadn't opened in twenty years; good insulation, maybe, but the important stuff, hell, he remembered enough of that.

"Now about this paper work," she says.

He studies his thin fingers, the mismatched size of each knuckle. "I love all your generation," he says, at near-murmur volume. She glances down, turns a page, although he can tell she isn't reading. He lets a hiccup of time pass, and then he says, "I love your persistence."

"Thank you, sir," she says, showing just a hint of weariness in her voice.

"What do you think of this room?" He considers raising a hand in an expansive gesture, but dismisses it as gratuitous. "A real bare-bones kind of a place, don't you think? Almost not the kind of thing you'd expect. Almost rustic."

"Yes, it's definitely that."

"I like to come here and think."

"Senator. The paperwork."

"Of course. Of course."

He settles back into the chair, searching for something within his own head. A word to describe big government. Medicinal, that one comes closest. He likes the implications. Salves and ointments and small bits of surgery constantly propping up the body politic. The pinch of the overused needle drawing blood and taxes.

Occasionally, when he sits in this room long enough, he thinks, somewhere, someone has gotten it right. They've thought the right thoughts at the right time. They've captured it, whatever it is. It's a thought that inspires and depresses him in alternating waves.

The knob turns, slowly, almost imperceptibly. Both the Senator and his assistant watch as the door slides open. His son, dressed in a coat and tie. A sign of an approaching protracted conversation. The Senator is surprised, actually, that it took him this long. The other children appeared the day before, en masse, each one more angry and confused than the one before. "Jimmy," the Senator says, "you grew a beard."

His son's hand wanders to his face, as if this was slightly alarming news to him. "Dad," he says. "You probably know why I'm here."

"Yes. Yes."

The words have the clumsy, community theater quality that comes with being observed by the disinterested, although the girl is politely watching everything but the two men: the open folder, the shoes on her feet. His son stands, holding his wet coat, first in one hand, then the other. He is the youngest of four by his second wife, and the senator can see it all over him, despite the beard: the way he looks from side to side before speaking, the thirty-five-year-old baby fat in his cheeks, the slight plead in his voice when he does say something. "Dad, is it true?"

What about truth, the Senator wants to say. The truth, it's a spatter of mercury. It's what you see when lightning flashes. It's whoever speaks loudest. I'm writing my own book, he wants to tell him. "It's a lie," he says. "It's all lies."

"What is?"

"All of it. Everything."

"Are you sure, Dad? Are you positive?"

"Yes. Of course."

"Are you absolutely positive?"

"I'm not absolutely positive of anything. I'm not absolutely positive you're standing in front of me now carrying on this ridiculous conversation."

"You know what I mean. I want to be sure. I want you to be sure."

The blanket across the senator's lap falls to the floor as he stands. "You're still my kid," he says. "I'm still your father." He takes his son by the wrist. He wants to show him something, a simple lesson. He begins to pull.

"Dad?"

With his other hand the senator reaches up and grips the back of his son's neck, where the skin is warm and moist. "Still your God damn father," he says, and he pulls harder, until he is breathing heavily. He lifts his foot and tries to place it against his son's knee, but instead it kicks and jerks, like the hind leg of a dog when its back is scratched. "God damn," he grunts. He imagines his son somersaulting over his shoulders, landing on the rug behind him; that's what you have to do when you want to accomplish something, imagine it through. He lets his body go limp, tries to drag his son to the floor.

"Dad? Are you okay?"

"Damn kid. God damn son-of-a-bitch kid."

"What's wrong?"

"Two-bit engineer. God damn bridge builder."

"Dad, what are you doing?"

The senator lets go and steps backward, his hands falling to his sides. "Nothing," he says.

They stand there, staring at each other. That's the curse of having children, the senator thinks, they get to see you die. He ponders the similarity in their quizzical expressions, in their genetic material, and makes a mental note to himself. This is a moment for the book. For one of the books. One for the books. What causes the human mind to move so quickly toward triteness?

But he feels the anger leaving him, the last vestige of its pale electric charge. He feels his mouth forming into a smile. "I'm starving. Let's go out to some stupid little restaurant," he says. "Let's get a piece of God damn pie." He decides it's time to be gratuitous. He raises both arms in a gesture that encompasses the entire contents of the room, including his assistant, who has taken another step deeper into her corner.

The Senator offers to pay for lunch, hoping this will be interpreted as a small concession, a thread's width close to an apology. He tries to will away the stitch in his side, the heaviness in his legs. He practices wiggling his toes. "You should roll down the window a little," his son says. "Get some fresh air."

"Sure," he says back, which is as much effort as he can muster.

At the restaurant the three of them are seated between two families. Children barely able to stay in their seats, food barely able to stay on the table. But the waitress is cute and the coffee is good.

The Senator has always been attracted by incongruity, and he likes that his son and his assistant look out of place here; meanwhile, he fits right in. Incognito, he thinks. A great word. Sounds like what it is. The girl, she picks up a fork and moves it around in her hand, scrapes it with her fingernail. The Senator takes in the awkwardness, orders coffee for everyone, as simple as holding up three fingers, then decides on ham and eggs with a side-order of sausage thrown in as an afterthought. The small rebellions are the most satisfying. "Well," the son says with a sigh, "who is the baton getting passed to?"

The senator concentrates on the coffee sliding down into the warmth at the base of his belly. It feels familiar and comforting. "I don't know about any baton," he says.

The son looks sideways at the assistant. "Really? I figured, you know."

The assistant sighs. "We haven't really discussed it. It's a timing thing. Windows of opportunity are constantly opening and closing depending on all sorts of factors. Moods. Whims." She rotates her cup thoughtfully. "You more than anyone probably know the drill."

"Yes," he says with a smile. "I know the drill. Do I ever know the drill."

"He's a difficult man to work for, your father. But an intelligent man. Unfocused, these days, but still pretty smart. And anyway, anyone can be smart. He has charisma. And he has longevity, of course. He's an icon, really, your father. If a movie were made of his life he'd be played by Charlton Heston."

The Senator feels like the guest on the talk show who hasn't walked onto the stage yet, who is still in the green room watching on the monitor. He wants to reach out and squeeze his son's face, gently but firmly, just to let him know he's here. He wants a blueberry muffin or at least some God damned cinnamon toast.

"The book's not going to undo all the good," the assistant says. "I won't let it. We won't let it. What it will do, after the initial media scramble, is add to the mystique. It makes him multi-dimensional, is what it does. If we handle it correctly. Which is to say that we aren't going to handle it all. I wouldn't touch this thing with a ten foot you-know-what."

"So it's a good thing?"

"I'm not saying that. I would never say that. It's actually an incredibly bad thing. A horrible, horrible thing. Especially now in the home stretch of his career. But I'm looking way down the road on this one. We'll go into retirement, which actually should have been done a few years back anyway, and then sit around, let the myth accrue."

"The myth."

"That's right. Do you think in the later stages of Muhammad Ali's career they were worried about whether he was going to win this individual fight or that individual fight? No, they were worried about the big historic picture, how all the pieces fit together. A failure can actually reinforce the victories." She sniffles just slightly. "Time is our ally on this one. Time has *always* been *his* ally." And she glances at the Senator and smiles, as if she has just paid him a slightly embarrassing complement. She is really quite pretty, he decides. She talks too much but she has nice large eyes. The Senator has always disliked small-eyed people.

"This is pretty good coffee," his son says thoughtfully, making room for the next subject.

"Yes," she says. "It is. It's actually very good."

Sometimes the Senator feels like embattled territory. People come and stake their claims and throw some elbows around and then move on to make room for someone else.

The coffee *is* good. He agrees with them on that.

Lunch arrives. The Senator notices how important food is in a good conversation. It fills the gaps, all the munch, munch, munch. It sustains the rhythm. Gives the people involved a common purpose.

The girl is smiling at one of his son's small jokes. The smile is fifty percent politeness, forty percent sincerity, ten percent something else.

She asks, "What was he like growing up?"

He says, "Inaccessible."

A man and a woman at the next booth are staring. Baseball cap and flannel shirt. The almost violent smear of catsup on hash browns. Teased hair. Basic working-class prototype guy and girl. Two weeks ago they would have been grinning raptly; they would have come over and said hello even. But they've read her paperback account of things, and they're wondering a little. Something's been stirred at the back of their brains. There are better ways you could have spent your ten bucks, he wants to tell them. Your seven bucks. Your twelve bucks. Whatever books cost nowadays. He sets down his knife and opens and closes his hand. Fist, palm, fist, palm.

What's the name of her God damned book again? He's burned enough of them, he should remember. *The Long Election? The Long Farewell? The Long Haul?* It wouldn't be quite so bad, if he could just remember. It's like trying to scratch a stupid little itch that keeps changing location. Scratching what you think is the right place *causes* it to become the wrong place. Thinking what you believe to be the right words *makes* them the wrong words.

His son asks the girl if she wants some of his omelet. If this is flirting, it's the worst the Senator has ever seen, but she nudges her plate over and the son slides half the omelet across, the cheese stretching briefly between them. "Thank you," she says.

"No problem."

"So what was your mother like?"

"Which one? My biological one or my stepmom?"

"Mom the author. The scandalous mom."

"My stepmom."

"That's the one."

"Strange. She was much younger than him, of course, so I think that had a lot to do with it. She was learning as she went along, I guess."

"We all do that. That's no kind of excuse."

"True. But she was capable of these bursts of affection." He shrugs. "Although so was he. There's this one time I remember vividly. It's a good story, but it wasn't included in the book, intentionally or not, I don't know."

"That's just the kind of thing the public needs to hear," she says, interrupting him. She likes the idea that such a story exists but she doesn't necessarily have to hear it. She looks around for the waitress, for the check. "We can't salvage everything, of course. The preemptive strike always wins in these situations. But we can at least step down gracefully. The old-fashioned man besieged by a new way of life decides the game has become too cutthroat. That kind of thing."

The Senator watches them from deep within himself. His vision is blurring in and out, and it is as if he is studying something distant and unknown: shadowy underwater tentacle-shapes. "I'm not stepping down," he says to the table edge. He has suddenly convinced himself. It will be a time for new directions anchored by old values. Maybe he should jump parties. Keep everyone guessing. Feint, jab, and feint. His right leg aches, just above the knee. Below the knee he is not so sure about.

"Be reasonable, Dad," the son says.

The Senator's words come out as a determined croak. "I have to do it." There are too many words on the tip of too many tongues. Too many reminiscences floating around in the ozone. Each day campaigning will be a day spent rewriting sentences from that damned book.

"But why?" the son shoots back, which dissolves the senator's brief fear that he has not been speaking loudly enough to be heard. He feels light-headed now, insubstantial. He rests both hands on the table and begins to push himself to his feet.

"I have to go," he says.

"Excuse me?"

"I have to go."

The Senator wanders off in the most likely direction. As he watches his feet lift and slide he decides, Yes, this is where it starts, the marathonlike campaign. There's no other choice, never was. Birds sing. Painters paint. He seeks re-election. "God damned wet floors," he mumbles to himself. He's not feeling very well. He's not feeling well at all.

There's something clean about a good bowel movement. You can feel it just below your stomach, the empty space to fill, the possibilities. For the full effect you have to stand up, turn around and stare it down in the bowl. You have to make that moment of connection. He finds a short hall with twin doors at the end, one next to the other. He rests his hand on the metal rectangular plate, pushes, and steps inside.

The first thing he sees is the girl kneeling on the floor, tying her shoe. A small oriental girl with a boy's haircut, a boy's T-shirt. For all he knows it might be a boy. But no, the voice belongs to a girl. "You're not supposed to be in here," she says, in a voice that is flat and accusatory and more than a little daunting.

"What?"

"You're not supposed to be in here."

His fingers hover around the zipper of his pants as he scans the blank tile, the three stalls, one oversized with a smooth metal railing. He makes a scraping noise at the back of his throat—then again—and moves forward by instinct.

"Hey, mister. What are you doing?"

He stops to consider this. A thought occurs to him: a nation's character can be judged solely by its rest rooms. He can imagine reams of statistical data supporting this small kernel, the sparks of discussion and cross-theorizing. A possible chapter heading. A book unto itself. He settles onto the seat, slacks around his ankles, and closes his eyes, *concentrating*. It hurts for him to urinate. It takes courage, fortitude. There is something profoundly sad about this.

The girl shouts from the other side of the wall. "Hey, you. You can't do that." He hears the thump of her small fist against the stall. What is she talking about? What did he ever do to her? "Hey, mister." The rhythmic clatter of the lock rattling, baby-fist pounding. "Mister!"

He doubles over, fixes on the knot in his stomach, and hopes she will go away. She does go away; he goes away, down into himself. A pain splits him from crotch to chest. It might be indigestion. Her voice is receding, turning from demand to plea as he gasps and lurches to one side. My third heart attack, he realizes, almost calmly, and all of a sudden it's as if he's seen it coming on all day, slowly moving closer, like a train. Or that barn in the distance. In the cold, growing larger, somehow occupying the space inside him.

"Mister?" The pit-pat of small feet moving away.

His face feels cool and yielding against the metal. The toilet paper dispenser acts as a head rest. It comes to him then, a dim awareness. The creep, creep of knowing. This is where they will find him, any second, in this room. He knows where he is now, and that this is where his history begins. Such a simple mistake. A punch line. Not what he wants, obviously.

He sees the faded blur of sandblasted graffiti, the dirty hieroglyphics pressed against his face. The usual words for the usual orifices. Ridiculous teenaged rants. A phone number and a name. Drawings and scribbles and the scratched sentence, *Please stop writing here*, and another beneath it, *Ok I will.*

A word near his cheek, another above his head, the third along his eye. His pupil moves along it, caresses it, flickering, taking it all in.

THE FORGOTTEN KINGDOM

THE COMPANY HAD BEEN LINGERING on the edge of death for almost three months. More and more boxes piled up in the halls as offices became empty spaces. Two of the three receptionists had been let go, and most of the engineers, and all but one of the salespeople. The remaining employees—mostly technical support and a few production people who would disappear as soon as they met their deadlines—had begun to casually scavenge the half-vacant space. Hard drives, memory cards, and monitors had been vanishing for quite a while and the building's overall mood felt similar to the half-controlled greed at a really good yard sale.

But Denny limited himself to the felt-tipped pens he liked so much and paper from the copy machine—things he had taken since he had started work here just under a year ago and which he felt were fair compensation for having one of the floor's smallest and most out-of-the-way cubicles. Even though there were three empty offices behind him, when he asked his boss if he could move she sighed and looked at him as if he had just revealed himself as selfish and petty.

"Denny," she said. "Is this really important considering everything that's going on?"

So each day Denny sat in that cramped cubicle, dispensing phone advice to people who were playing the company's video games. He ate candy bars and threw the balled-up wrappers at the trash, muttering to himself if he missed especially badly. Sometimes he let the phone ring five, six, seven times before answering, his hand hovering just above the receiver.

"Hello," he'd finally say when he answered, his voice Disneyland-friendly. "Praxis Software Hint Line."

The office was particularly quiet today, as if someone had called a holiday and hadn't informed him, and Denny was bored out of his mind, so much so that he was almost relieved when the phone began to buzz. "Hello," he said automatically, but the voice interrupted him before he could finish his recitation.

"Yeah," a nervous voice on the other end said. "I'm in this dungeon."

"What game are you playing?" Denny asked, although he remembered. This guy was a regular. He could tell from the familiar, halting way he talked, and the phlegmy quality to his voice—the way he made a small, thoughtful puckering sound at the end of a sentence, as if he were blowing small kisses. Sometimes he called two or three times a day.

"What?" the man asked.

"What game are you playing?"

"*Warriors*. The one with the demon on the box cover."

"*Warriors of the Forgotten Kingdom*," Denny said. It was at least three years old, ancient by industry standards. All the games from back then had long pretentious names, as if you were getting more for your dollar if the title had more than twenty letters. Now the games were all single word—*Pyre, Cruise, Destroyer*—cool and efficient. An ultra-Darwinian vibe—only a few of the very strongest survived. To Denny more and more things seemed Darwinian lately. "And what dungeon are you in?" he asked.

70

"Well, the walls are yellow," the man said. "I had to use the Key of Skulls to get in."

Denny punched "Key of Skulls" into his database. "You're in the goblin dungeon," he said. "Near the Mountains of Malice."

"Yeah," the guy said, as if Denny had only confirmed what he already knew. "Well, there's this underground river. It's on fire."

Denny laboriously plugged the key words in. River. Fire. Underground. "The River of Living Flame," he said, when the answer scrolled across his screen.

"Yeah, well, I can't figure out how to cross it. I always die."

"You always die," Denny said to himself. "Okay." He clicked some more, digging deeper into the near-limitless pile of help files on his computer. "Do you have the Stone of Frost?" he finally asked, trying to sound as disinterested as possible.

"The what?"

"It's in the mountains."

"What mountains?"

"The Mountains of Malice."

"Oh," the man said. "Thanks," and he hung up. Denny minimized the database and toggled to his e-mail, which was empty except for a couple of generic junk messages. He had nothing better to do so he took out one of his black pens and began to doodle in his notebook. He liked to draw small, violent pictures—people screaming and children with wild, angry eyes. Word balloons containing filthy, chicken-scratched language. His mother told him once they were drawings a crazy person would make, which stung for a second, but now he considered it a compliment. In art school he had even published some of them, including the ones his mother had seen, in a Xeroxed fanzine and he had received some acclaim and more infamy.

But now that he had dropped out, cartooning was just a diversion. He folded the half-finished drawing and put it in the bottom drawer of his desk, where he hoped someone would find it when he was gone.

The phone didn't ring again for the next hour, despite Denny's feeling that any second it was going to buzz and the trivia of someone else's life would force its way into his. There were long droughts like this, in which Denny began to feel strangely ignored. Finally he stood and spent some time exploring the computer in the next cubicle. The person who once worked at that station had left his hard drive packed with sound files—chipmunk voices swearing, snippets of movies and television shows. The computer seemed like a depository of the entire mass culture, reduced to more than a hundred short catch phrases that you could click on and play and delete and generally just fuck around with. A lesson in secrets, Denny decided, because the man who had worked at that station always looked neat and efficient, and not like the kind of person who would spend his time doing something like Denny was doing now. Eventually, when he realized he had been bored for a long time, Denny microwaved leftover curried vegetables for an early dinner and sat in the break room, complaining to the only other guy who seemed to be left in the building.

"It's ridiculous," Denny told him.

The guy seemed to be listening. At least he nodded his head as he pushed his food around, mumbling something that sounded like angry agreement. Denny had never seen him before and most likely would never see him again.

"The higher-ups," Denny said, "they send out all these nice, flowery memos but they don't care about us." The company had stopped filling the soda machines two weeks ago. It was a perfect sign that the mucky-mucks weren't even trying to fight the rigor mortis. "It's like we're in a Third World country," Denny said. The man grunted and poked at his chicken salad.

Denny dropped his yellowed Styrofoam dish into the trash and took a walk around the empty halls, looking over the sayings on people's coffee mugs and the notes on their calendars. He opened their drawers, hoping to find something distinct and a little exciting, but he only found the usual paperclips and Post-it notes. He did this for a good twenty minutes, keeping an ear open for the phone, and he didn't see another person. It was always like this in the early evening.

His phone was buzzing again. He thought briefly about not picking it up, or picking it up and then slamming it down. He often felt this way when he was more-or-less alone here—almost untouchable, like the captain of a gauzy ghost ship—but he considered himself smart enough to resist the stray impulses.

"Hello," he said. "Praxis Software Hint Line." And then, on a whim, as a concession to the defiant feeling, and just to puncture the bubble of protective anonymity, "Denny speaking."

"I'm in a very big swamp."

It was him again. Was he was the only one out there in the world?

The man explained his situation quietly, but with something similar to real distress in his voice. He was headed in the wrong direction, Denny realized, toward the Ogre Citadel. Or was it the Crystal Kingdom? He thought of going to his computer and punching it up and seeing what came back, but then he thought, why bother? "You have to go north," he said. "Do you have a compass?"

"Oh," he said. "North. Thanks," he said, but his breathing seemed to hang on the line. "I'm sorry I call so often," he finally said. "You're probably very busy."

73

"Not really," Denny said noncommittally. But he had to admit he had given him an invitation in the way he had answered the phone. Still, he wasn't quite used to seeing the people who called him as completely human and he assumed that they should pay him the same courtesy.

"It's a hard game. It can be very frustrating." He laughed. "Yesterday, I almost punched the monitor screen."

"Yeah, well," Denny said. "It was meant to be difficult."

"It's definitely that. I just feel I take a lot of your attention."

"Actually," Denny said. "We're in the process of shutting down now so we all have a lot of free time on our hands." He felt like he was giving the man what he wanted, a simple little absolution. He was like one of those old ladies you hear about, talking to phone solicitors about their cats.

"What was that?" the man asked.

"We're shutting down," Denny said. "Going out of business."

"When is that going to happen?"

"Pretty soon probably."

"I was kind of counting on finishing the game," the man said, and he paused and seemed to be thinking about something. Denny could hear his breathing. Then he said, "Are you going to continue your 800 service after you close down? Some places do that."

"No," Denny said. "Not video game companies. Not us, anyway. I'm just going to disappear. Poof. That's it. History." He was turning the screws a little now, he knew, but he couldn't help it.

"Well," the man said. "I'll probably talk to you a little later," and again his breathing seemed to hang there.

"Good-bye," Denny said, and he snuffed out the connection with the tap of his finger.

By eight o'clock that night he had decided to head home early, a risk he allowed himself once or twice a week. On the way out he passed someone he recognized coming in—a fellow second shift worker arriving late. But this man was running more than six hours behind. That seemed gluttonous—even considering the office behavior of late—and Denny couldn't help but say, "Have a good night," with an edge in his voice as he held the door for him.

The night air was cool but he had his hooded sweatshirt in his knapsack. He unlocked his bicycle and coasted down the long, landscaped hill and into the street. He bent low into the peddling, the occasional set of headlights moving up behind and then strobing over him as the car passed.

"It's dangerous," his mother had told him, back when she still talked about the outside world, and yes, he could have used her Toyota. She certainly wasn't using it. But these rides were the most interesting part of his day—he liked the cramped streets, the broken sidewalks, and the surly drivers. Occasionally people yelled at him from their windows. Once someone even threw a half-eaten cheeseburger.

Denny had spray-painted his bike silver and gold—rims included—and he took pride in hearing them mock the way it looked, the way *he* looked as he waved his hand for them to pass. Then he raised his fist in salute so they could see it in their rearview mirror, not so much as an insult, just a simple form of communication, his way of saying, *You keep doing what you're doing and I'll keep doing what I'm doing.* Tonight he would have enjoyed even that brief contact, because the last phone conversation had left him feeling especially restless. And so he pumped his legs faster until he could feel the sweat on the back of his neck. The streets, he realized, were wet. It had rained while he was working.

He picked up more curry at a boxlike little restaurant where he often ate. Eating there was satisfying on many levels. The food they served was semi-exotic and he had to head into a bad neighborhood to pick it up. The vegetables snapped between his teeth, which gave him an odd sense of accomplishment when he chewed.

When the man behind the counter wrote down what Denny wanted—small ticks and scribbles that could have been numbers, could have been a foreign language—Denny sat at the place's only table, a greasy wood grain plastic square with a television suspended from the wall just behind it. It seemed like the man at the counter was staring at him, and although he knew he was just watching two masked wrestlers beat each other silly, it was still somehow unsettling. He opened a newspaper someone had left behind and leafed through it, not reading, but taking in the layout, the pictures, the general shape.

"Good night," the man behind the counter said, when he handed over the small brown bag, receipt stapled efficiently to the top flap.

"You too," Denny said. Although he came here a couple of times a week they never exchanged more than these simple words.

He placed the bag into his backpack, pulled up his hood and yanked the strings, and headed down the street toward the empty intersection. He paused there even though there was no traffic, his weight balanced on one foot, and he wondered if people were always supposed to feel this relaxed and confident. There was a gas station up ahead and a small neighborhood grocery store—neither familiar. He banged a wide U-turn and headed back where he had come from, underneath a bridge covered with primitive spray painted designs. On particularly bleak evenings like this one it seemed as if civilization had ended mysteriously and quietly. He had somehow survived and he was figuring out what he should do. The idea was both repulsive and attractive and he liked to play around with it in his head in the same way he had played with the belongings of his absent co-workers.

The scenery became unfamiliar again—a narrow bar with a lit Budweiser sign, a parking lot with a chain across the entrance, some darkened warehouses. He slowed and moved into another wide U-turn. All of a sudden he knew where he was headed. Eventually he was going to end up parked in front of her house, just like Tuesday and Sunday of last week, and the Thursday before that. Funny how the realization still caught him off guard.

It was late when he pulled up her street. It had taken him a while to find his way, and he had stopped at a 7-Eleven for an overpriced Gatorade the color of a bug light. The curry was still uneaten, but it was holding its warmth pretty well. At one intersection he had touched his knapsack almost tenderly, pushing down until he could feel the heat from the takeaway bag.

Her neighborhood seemed to have been designed by a kind, unimaginative man, possibly in a single sitting. The lawns were green and large and almost uniform. The streets were wide enough for children to play in and at the end of one street stood a park where Denny used to smoke pot not so long ago.

The rain returned after five or ten minutes, just a light drizzle that felt good on his face. Soon the water would begin to collect in small rivers at the edge of the sidewalk. The next day the children would kneel there, watching the water drain off into the sewer grate. Denny, of course, would be soaked, but he didn't mind.

Most of the homes were dark, and in those that weren't, only a single light or two shone from a bedroom or kitchen. He noticed the blue square of a television screen through the picture window across the street, and he tried in vain to see if he could figure out what program the people who lived there were watching. When he looked back at her house the porch light was burning, although maybe it had been that way before and he hadn't noticed. And as he told himself, Yes, that must be it, the door opened and she stepped outside.

"Hello, Denny," she said, as she moved halfway down the porch stairs. She was dressed in a bathrobe with a brown rain slicker wrapped around her shoulders and her hair was tied back in a small pony tail. He wondered if this was a new style for her. He couldn't remember her ever wearing it that way, although maybe he just never noticed. A little conservative, he decided, but he liked it.

"Hello, Caroline," he said. "It's raining."

"Thanks," she said, and she glanced at the sky, as if to say, "You know, you're right, it is." But she didn't move to invite him in or even go inside herself. "I could have woken my parents, you know," she finally said.

"I'm very glad you didn't," he said. He clicked the gears on his bike, rocking back and forth slightly as if preparing for a race that might start any second. It had been more than a month and he was still taken aback to see her.

"How's your mother doing?" she asked. "I hope she's well."

He was not so stupid as to believe he loved Caroline. They had dated off and on in high school and into the first few months of college but had finally decided to break up for good more than a year ago, during a long and slightly apathetic dinner conversation he had initiated. He remembered telling her, "I really need to concentrate on my work," and squeezing her hand gently when she began crying.·

During the breakup she spoke of finding herself by backpacking across Europe or getting a job in some remote part of the country, so Denny was both pleased and disappointed to find her living at her parents' house when he returned to town. When they dated she had maps all over her bedroom walls, even the ceiling, and she often took him by the hand and pointed out the black dots representing Greek and Italian cities. Denny was sure that the maps were now on the wall of her new bedroom—her old childhood bedroom—and that sureness made him want to ask her if she was hungry. They'd watch the rain like they were watching a drive-in movie, curry between them, sharing the one plastic fork.

"I'm not really sure how she's doing," he said, and he realized this made it sound as if he had not seen her lately, so he added, "Sometimes she seems pretty good," and then he shrugged, because he didn't know what to say at all. "Caroline, we should go out to lunch sometime," he finally added, although the words sounded foolish, and he didn't really want to do that with her anyway. He was content to talk with her here.

She laughed. "What are we doing? You're out here on your magical golden bicycle in the rain and you're asking me to lunch." She stopped and then laughed some more, and then he laughed too—it was that ridiculous—and then she said, "Who's coming by the house these days?"

"A nutritionist, once in a while, and three health aides, one in the morning, one in the afternoon, and then one at dinnertime when I'm not there. The first two look almost exactly the same. Completely interchangeable. And they're so old I wonder if my mother should be taking care of them." They laughed again, and she turned and looked at her house. When she turned back to him her expression was serious, her lips a thin line, her eyes tired somehow. Maybe he did love her. Maybe he *was* that stupid. He looked down at his hands and said, "I don't understand her."

"What do you mean?"

"Well, she paints now. All these nature scenes and horses and these little white houses." He stood on his pedals and then pushed into motion, moving in a small circle to the other side of the street and then returning to exactly the same spot he had been a few seconds before—next to Caroline. "Miss me?" he asked.

She ignored that last question and said, "It helps her."

She didn't know what he meant. How could she, when he didn't exactly know either? "She's always so happy," he said. "She sings these little songs. She sits there with a paint brush in her hand going la-la-la, la-la-la." He was almost on the verge of making fun of her, he thought, like when he was a kid and she brought him to the grocery store and he walked just behind her, imitating her slow walk, the way she lifted and inspected a grapefruit.

"Don't worry," Caroline said, which is what people resorted to when they were at a loss. But then she brightened unpredictably and touched the handlebars of the bike with extended fingers, as if she were checking to see if it were real. Then she dropped her hand to her side, smiling, her eyes scanning the painted frame, the spray painted silver rings, as if counting them. She looked back at the house again and said, "But this is the last time, right Denny?"

"What do you mean?"

"I've seen you out here before," she said. "How many times has it been?"

"Three," he said.

But something had burned itself out, now that he had seen her up close, and he guessed that the number wouldn't grow any larger. He could feel it and he guessed that Caroline could probably feel it too, and that she was probably a little sad and a little relieved.

"Good-bye," she said. "Take care."

"You too," he said.

Someone was standing at the edge of the street, a plastic grocery bag in each hand, a black knit cap pulled down tightly over his bowed head. The bags, the number 22 on the back of the jacket—the figure was so symmetrical as to seem premeditated—a self-contained grubby little nomad. Denny disrupted the picture with a loud, "Look out!" as he sped past, but when he turned and looked over his shoulder the man was still watching the sidewalk.

It was still raining the next day, and on the way to work Denny had to fight the urge to head across town. Caroline wouldn't be home—she was probably counting out crisp new dollar bills to another customer and thinking about her lunch break—but there was something else Denny wanted. The desire reminded him of eating a big dinner and thinking that you'll never eat again, then waking the next morning with an even worse appetite.

When he had come home the night before, he had found his mother twisted on the living room fold-out bed, legs splayed and hands pulled closely to her chest. The blankets and the foam bed pad had been rumpled up and kicked to the bottom of the mattress. There was a kind of violence in the way she slept, Denny thought. Her frail hands were always shut tight, and sometimes she knocked over the water pitcher on the nightstand. He didn't know how. It seemed like you'd have to go out of your way to do something like that. He bent down and picked up the pad and shook it out a little.

"Denny?" she asked.

"Go back to sleep," he said.

Her voice grew more demanding. "Denny?"

She opened her eyes, but he knew she couldn't see him. He was standing at her feet and she was looking out into the kitchen, at the small night light shining to one side of the toaster oven. Past the light stood one of her unframed paintings, splashes of happy yellows and blues and the brown square of a beach house. The house itself was unfinished and so was the painting and this double incompleteness seemed strangely profound. Too long a glance at one of these paintings—the remote triangular mountains, the equally triangular and frozen-looking waves—and a murky queasiness lodged itself in his center. "I'm over here, Mom," he said.

Her head turned in his general direction. He could see her but he knew she still couldn't really see him. "Denny," she said, in a disappointed way. "What were you doing tonight?" And then, before he could answer, "I need something to sip on." She coughed lightly, as if in explanation.

"Sure," he said, and poured her some water. He helped her sit up and then handed her the small plastic cup. She took it in both hands, but she didn't drink.

She had survived two marriages, a tedious job in the cramped payroll office of a shoe factory, and a score of lesser disasters including, Denny decided, his own adolescence and young adulthood. A year ago when she was first diagnosed it seemed like she would survive this too, but lately he was less and less sure. "Basquiat from heroin," she said evenly. "Van Gogh did it himself, of course." He had heard this before. He looked at the small digital clock she kept on the night stand with all her other supplies. It was almost two in the morning. "I'm sure you know the Norwegian expressionist Edvard Munch. You wouldn't think someone like that would live a long life, would you? What do you think of him?"

"Hush," he said, and she nodded and drank. He could hear her throat work. Then she handed him the empty cup and he put it back on the nightstand.

Although he did not have to be in until the afternoon he set his alarm for ten. In his mind he was checking off the things he would do in the morning—the shave, the shower—as he undressed and dropped his clothes in bundles on the floor. He climbed into bed and put his arm over his eyes. With his arm like that he could hear his watch ticking close to his ear and he started to count the seconds, which is how two o'clock became two-thirty, and then three, and then he was awake, the radio playing loud dance music. He had slept through the alarm. It was almost eleven. He reached out and slapped the noise away and swung his legs around.

Denny tried to log-on to the computer when he got to work but he had forgotten his password again. He opened his desk and began to look for the scrap of paper where he had written it, rain dripping from his hair onto the desk calendar. As he rummaged around a person walking by went out of her way not to look at him. He had never seen her before. She was skulking around inspecting boxes and making checks on a clipboard with a stubby pencil. As a portent, she wasn't a good sign of things to come.

The phone began to buzz, three times, then five. He let it tire itself out. It stopped on the sixth ring, or was rerouted somewhere else in the system, to some other desk somewhere. He listened for the ringing to change location but didn't hear anything but the hum of the florescent lights and a conversation over by the copiers, something about one football team devastating another one. The phone rang again. He picked it up on the fourth ring, partly out of curiosity, partly just to shut it up. "Hello," he said. "Praxis Software Hint Line."

"Denny?" the voice said slowly. "Is that you? That is you, Denny, isn't it?"

"Who is this?" he asked, although he knew.

"Denny, I need help," the man said, in his thick voice, and he sighed, as if he was disappointed in himself and knew Denny would be too. Denny could hear the man's breathing in the pause before he said, "I'm in the Glade of Vampire Ravens. Near all of those glass towers." The man seemed to think about this and then he chuckled in his nervous way. "Don't ask me how I got here." Denny let the silence linger. It settled comfortably into place. The men at the copy machine had stopped talking. "What should I do?" the man asked.

"What's your name?" Denny asked.

"Mike," the man said, after a short pause.

"Well, Mike, here's the best advice I can give you. Stop playing the game. Just give up." He opened his free hand in a gesture of release and immediately felt embarrassed by his own theatricality.

"I really want to finish the game, Denny," Mike said. "You told me yourself, there's not much time left." Another clipped laugh. "I need to pump you for as much information as I can."

Denny switched the phone to his other ear. "Jesus," he said. "I'd say you've completed only about thirty percent so far, and you've been playing for a long time." He was standing now, the phone cord twined snakelike around his arm.

"I know that," the man said. "Don't you think I know that?

Sometimes I want to break the disc into pieces and force feed it to the guy who came up with the stupid thing." He laughed nervously. "That probably sounds a little crazy to you."

"No, not really," Denny admitted. He felt as if he were zeroing in on something small and faraway and when the man said that he had embarrassed himself and that he should probably get going, he said, "Wait a second," because he hadn't quite zeroed in completely. But the line was dead.

That night he ate Chinese food while sitting on the curb across the street from Caroline's house.

Early the next morning he found three five-dollar bills in the inner pocket of his jean jacket. This was one way he and his mother communicated lately—she sometimes left money there, crisp and dry, like leaves. He put the cash into his wallet and pledged to spend it on something he didn't need.

"I'm going now," he called out to her as he left the house by the back porch. "Don't read too much, okay?"

He had left his bicycle on the porch the night before and it had fallen over sometime during the night, wedging itself against the door. He jerked and pushed but the door would only open a few inches, so he cut back into the house, heading toward the front door. "What's the matter?" his mother called out, but he didn't answer except to wave. Her bed was piled with oversized library art books.

"C'mon, we have a busy day," he said, as he wrestled his bicycle free from the door at the rear of the house. He half-pushed, half-carried it down the steps, kicking himself into motion at the top of the driveway.

He headed in the direction of the mall, where the interstate brushed up against the edge of the city. He hadn't been there in a long time, because he was usually opposed to malls as a matter of principle, but he was looking forward to its bland cleanliness now. The last time he had gone there, four or five years ago, he had been trying to help his mother with one of her vague quests. The daughter of a woman she used to work with was getting married soon and although the wedding was in upstate New York, which meant she would not be going, she wanted to send something bright and expensive in lieu of her presence. The daughter was on the older side, approaching her mid-thirties, cause for extra celebration and an extra-special gift. Something really nice, his mother kept saying, a phrase that started out hopeful and almost frivolous and became tense and hungry as they exhausted possibilities. They wandered from store to store, Denny just ahead or just behind. Occasionally his mother called him over for an opinion on some fragile little thing she held in her hand, until they found themselves at the desolate far end of the mall, standing in front of a closed-down Sears and a cheese-and-cracker shop that occasionally gave away free samples. This is where Denny turned to her and told her, "Who gives a shit about any stupid gift anyway? It's not like she knows who you are."

He wanted to talk about that now, although he didn't necessarily want to apologize. He could picture that scene: face-to-face with his mother, trying to say the words, trying to make her remember the small damages shared between them—and he told himself that this wasn't what he wanted, what either of them wanted. But he did want to find somebody else and share the story with them. He wanted to at least do that. And then he would look into the person's face as he finished and gauge their reaction and have a better idea of what kind of person he was.

They had rebuilt the place in the last few years and he was

surprised how different it looked—twice as tall with a three-story parking deck. It looked like the kind of place a person could get lost in. And anyway it was too early in the morning. It wasn't even open yet, he realized. He looped around it once, coasting most of the way, occasionally zigzagging nonchalantly to avoid a broken bottle or even a crack in the pavement. The ground was still wet and on the way out of the parking lot he lifted both feet in the air and crashed through a deep puddle.

"Hi, Caroline," he said, when she came to the door after the fourth knock. There were, indeed, children playing in the street. Well, one child, a little boy in a yellow rain slicker. He was filling a small squirt gun with water from a muddy puddle, his face a mask of seriousness. "Cute kid, huh?" he said, but either she didn't agree or didn't care, because she only glanced very quickly at the kid before looking back at Denny. "Do I need a reason?" Denny said when she asked him why he had come back to her house and then, after a few seconds of silence in which it became clear she wouldn't be opening the door, "I didn't wake you up, did I?"

"Denny," she said. "I don't know what you want."

"I just want to talk." He was on the verge of telling her about his mother and their long ago trip to the mall, but for some reason he asked, "Did you like the drawings I used to do?" And then, "You used to say you liked them but I was never sure. I thought that maybe you were just saying that because we were, you know, dating."

"Denny, I have to go to work in a half-hour," she said. And then, in a voice just as level as the one she had used to describe her job, "I'm not very happy with my life right now, not at all, and you're not making it any easier."

"It's okay," he said, and he put his hand to the screen door, as if to calm her. It felt as flimsy as string, and made a satisfying metallic sound as he ran his fingers down it. He could see a few small holes large enough to poke a thumb through. "It's fine. I'll be going now. I'm going," but he didn't move, except to slide his hand up and down the screen in a padding doglike motion. This was how he was going to be remembered by her, he realized.

"You should go, Denny," she said. "You really should."

He said, "I will. I will," but he didn't. He moved his face closer to the screen, as if he wanted to kiss her through the wire, but that's not what he wanted, was it? And as he moved closer it was another face that appeared in the screen door—Caroline's father, his hand extended forward just as Denny's was, palm open and fingers wide. He opened the door just as Denny stepped back. "Denny, you get away from here," he said in a steady voice. He wore pajamas with a pattern of blue boats on them and he would have been a laughably ridiculous sight if he wasn't so angry. "Caroline is upset and she's scared. Can't you see that?"

He was quicker than he looked. He reached out to grab Denny, or to push him away, and Denny took another step back. His heel found no footing—just empty air—and suddenly he was spilling down the stairs. He struck the ground and then rose up into a crouch, feeling simultaneously clumsy and agile. His jeans were torn and gravel stuck to his skin around his knee. He paused there for a moment as if he might orate from that position—on his injured knee, hand extended—and then he uncoiled with a groan. As he stood he had to remind himself that he had tripped, not been pushed, and that the ache in his leg was probably nothing more than a shallow cut, and that none of what had just happened deserved any kind of retribution. Caroline's father loomed at the top of the stairs, his hands balled into fists but sympathy in his eyes. Denny wanted to jump up those stairs two at a time and, well, something would happen then, wouldn't it? It would have to. But instead he walked back toward his bicycle, wiping a bloody palm on his jeans.

At home he took a bath, reclining so that the water moved up past his ears, his face a small island in the tub. There was something luxurious about taking a bath in the daytime, and he remained immersed for a long time, feeling the water cool around his belly. There are things you have to do, he told himself. You need to buy a shirt and a dark jacket and pants and a tie. You need to change the name on the utilities. You need to get a good night's sleep. Each idea seemed overwhelming. He wanted someone to take him by the hand and lead him through each and every simple chore. Maybe that was another reason why he had gone by Caroline's again. He wanted to ask her help with the simple things. Although it also occurred to him that he had gone there specifically to hurt her, to make her feel a small fragment of what his mother must have been feeling, what he was feeling. He didn't know why. Maybe he was just a bad person. That seemed like a possibility.

He clicked the drain open with his big toe and let the water swirl away but even when it was gone he remained there, feeling the cool evaporation on his skin. He began to play with himself, concentrating on different women he had seen on television lately, but he gave up after a minute or two. He stood up and wrapped a towel around his waist and walked into the hall, close enough to the living room that he could see his mother but far enough away that there was no danger of waking her. The health aid had already arrived—he could hear the spoon clicking in the glass as she stirred magnesium into his mother's orange juice.

There was a new painting on the easel. This one was incomplete but it appeared to be a lighthouse with seagulls in the distance. The image bled away into pure white at the bottom of the canvas. There was something serene about the blankness and for a second he imagined that the bottom was the actual picture—that his mother was painting over all the blue and red and black and when it was finished it would be beautiful. "Mom," he said, and then louder, "Mom."

Her eyes flickered open. "Denny?" she said. "What's the matter?" He stood frozen until her eyes closed and her breath returned to its uneven sawing.

Denny waited for the call most of that evening. At around eight, when everyone had already gone home and he was scratching his third or fourth failed doodle out of existence, the phone finally rang. He answered it with just a clipped "Hello," because he knew.

"Well," Mike said. "I'm back at the same place."

"Near the Ogre Citadel?"

"The Ogre Citadel."

"Go east," Denny said. "You'll get to a fork in the road. Go left at the fork. Left. Then I'll tell you what to do next."

"Thanks," Mike said, and Denny listened to the hiss in the line as the man clicked his way out of the glade and back into the forest. "Now what?"

"Go until you reach a stone wall with a door in the side. Rummage around in the bush to its right until you find a copper key. Put the key in the lock and open the door and go in. Go straight until you get to the intersection. Take another left and then a right." He scanned through the information in his database. "Then another right."

"Okay," the man said, after a while. "Now what?"

"You're almost there," Denny said.

It was as if Denny was merely relating a long story to this other man, a story in which every action had a simple and clear effect. It was almost inspirational in its own plodding way and although they weren't even close to its inevitable ending, they were close enough for Denny to sigh and say, "I'm not sure how to put this."

"Go ahead," the man said, a little impatiently. Something had been reversed.

"Okay," he said, but he really didn't know how to put it—how to place the words into some kind of order that made sense. "A lot has been happening with me lately," he finally said, and he laughed. He tried to imagine where he would be a year from now and had no idea, just that it would be a very different place. But then he caught himself and remembered where they were right now, on the verge of a very small room that was one in a series of many small rooms. "Okay, let's see," he said as he oriented himself, and then they continued.

A heavy grinding reverberated from the next floor up—a dragging from one corner of the room toward the elevators on the other side of the building. The noise grew and then abated and then grew again and he hunched and cupped his ear to block it out. Up above his bent head they were taking things away.

WHAT WE OWN

<hr>

"YOU'RE SO SKINNY," MY FATHER SAID. "I should sue every officer in your unit. I should get a good lawyer and drag them into court."

"I'm okay," I told him. He was always threatening to sue neighbors, bosses, and rude sales clerks. It was like a gun he took out and showed you and waved around his head without firing.

We had just driven two hours from the airport, and although it was late, my father decided that I needed food more than sleep, and so the kitchen filled with the scent of onions and garlic while he opened and closed drawers, looking for spatulas, bowls, and cheese graters. "God knows how your mother can find anything in this mess," he said, although my mother was sitting right there at the table with me.

According to her, I didn't eat the meal he made me that night—I just poked it with my fork as I listened to him talk—but I remember how the food tasted. It was better than I had expected, and I was as relieved to be home as I had been to leave six months before.

"It looks delicious," I said, when he put the broken omelet down in front of me.

"The secret is a little bit of cream cheese," he said, as if this were something only the two of us were going to share. "Do you want anything else? Do you want some toast? We have rye bread."

"I don't think he's that hungry," my mother said. She was

folding and unfolding a paper napkin. To this day she talks about how he blackened her best pots, broke a bowl that had belonged to her great aunt.

"Tim's sleeping?" I asked.

"He wanted to stay up and see you, of course," she said, as she glanced at the ceiling, at his room hidden above our heads. "But he has school in the morning."

"He'll have plenty of time to visit you tomorrow afternoon," my father said, as he brought the pan over to the sink and poured hot water on it. "He's doing even worse lately, if you can believe that. Discipline problems too. I have to hear about it everyday in the teacher's lounge. God, am I sick of that chatter. You would think people would mind their own business."

My father had taught high school math for more than twenty years and he talked about his retirement as if it were something faraway and rainbow-colored. If I don't drop dead of a stroke first, he liked to say, holding up two fingers like some kind of prayer or salute, and my mother would send a little scowl his way, as if he were a child making just a little too much noise.

I finished eating and while my mother washed the dishes my father put out a bowl of Cheerios with a plate over the top as a lid. Then he checked the kettle for water and poured some Folgers into a coffee mug, leaving it by the bowl. "This is what I have to do," he said, "or getting up in the morning seems too much for me. I'm really lurching toward the finish line, Scott."

"If he could," my mother said, "he'd dress in his suit and tie before he went to bed," and in the quiet way my father laughed I could tell it was a joke he had heard often.

After they headed upstairs I leafed through a stack of recent copies of the thin local newspaper, and as I did that, I headed back in time, three days, and then five, then ten.

There was an article about little league baseball and tips about staying cool in the summer and an opinion piece about an over budget construction project. There were also UPI articles relegated to the back page of the first section—stories about murders, disasters in foreign countries, and strange shifts in the political wind—and I thought about how safe this town felt, how insulated from the world.

Eventually Tim appeared in the doorway. He was dressed in a dark T-shirt and jeans with torn-out knees. He had grown his hair longer—so that it fell into his eyes—and dyed it ink-black. The only thing that wasn't dark about him, I realized, was his skin, which was pale, almost translucent, like the skin of small, exotic fish. It had been almost half a year since I had seen him last and I had to fight the instinct to ask him, What's the matter?

"I figured you'd make an appearance tonight," I said. "It's good to see you."

"Yeah," he said. "You too," and he sat in the chair across from me, staring out from beneath his hair.

He knew what I was thinking, and he laughed a little before he said, "Dad calls it my disguise. He says I'm going to grow it all the way to my feet so nobody can see me."

"It bothers him, huh?"

"Nah. He doesn't care. He says as long as I clean the tub after I wash it."

"That's funny."

"I think he actually got into an argument with one of the other teachers about it. You know, defending me. I couldn't believe it. Mr. Cut-the-lawn-twice-a-week."

I smiled at that and I began to fold the paper back into order. Tim said, "Mom says you didn't do it intentionally. I mean, that you didn't mean to *actually* do it. You just used it as a way to get out." He grimaced and added, "You know what I mean." Although it wasn't cold out, he was putting on a coat, a black leather jacket with a thin racing stripe up one side. It was too small for him and instead of making him look tough, it made him look gawky and awkward.

"What does Dad say about it?"

"He doesn't say anything about it."

We said our good-byes and he left quietly, without turning on the porch light. I returned to what I'd been doing, leafing through almost a month's worth of papers stacked in the corner.

This is the day I decided to do it, I realized, when I found a newspaper from almost three weeks before. And this is when I did, I thought, when I found one from two days later, although of course it contained no news about what I had done to myself.

I felt almost sorry for the town, and everybody in it, my parents especially, because it could never be as safe and serene as anybody wanted it to be, including me.

I remember that first night sitting around the table, and the following Friday—the night my mother mentions most when she talks about that time—but the days between have blurred. Maybe they were a blur even then. During basic training every day had been as sharp and clear as cold water, and it was probably a relief to experience the days as hazy, billowy things, without direction or real purpose.

My father took over the kitchen for the entire week, making

lasagna and oversized salads, thick hamburgers with long slices of dill pickles and home fries. My mother refers to this as the week we had Thanksgiving everyday, but what I remember most is not the amount of food, but the sound of him preparing it. I sat in the living room, in his leather reclining chair, listening to him. I could hear the aggressive clatter of pots and pans, the occasional curse when he burned something or discovered he was missing a key ingredient.

He brought my food out to me on a tray and I'd eat while I watched quiz shows and cartoons. "What are you watching?" he'd ask quietly, and he would kneel down, rest his hand on the arm of the chair, and look at the screen with me, as if he was trying to see what I saw.

"*20,000 Dollar Pyramid*," I'd tell him. Or *The Bugs Bunny–Road Runner Hour* or *The Channel Fifty Early Movie*, depending on whether it was morning, afternoon, or evening.

"Is there anything you want to talk about?" he would say.

"I don't think so," I'd reply.

He would nod and frown thoughtfully. Then he would pat his knee and stand and smile and return to the kitchen, where he ate with my mother. Tim was usually upstairs during all of this. I could hear the dangerous-sounding thumping of his music through the floor.

"Why can't we eat as a family?" I often heard my father say to my mother. "One hour a day we could sit around the table and talk."

"It's a normal part of growing up," she told him.

"Well, let's be *abnormal*," he would reply. "This Friday we're all going to sit down and eat as a family, because that's what we are. A family. An *abnormal* family." That made him laugh loudly, and I remembered the times my mother had flinched at that laugh when we had been growing up. I could see her face, her eyes on a neutral corner of the room. As a kid, I had found a quiet place in some other part of the house when he raised his voice like that. Now he wanted us to sit around the kitchen table and talk about our lives.

What would I say? By what route had I arrived at this place, and where did I want to go next? The idea of trying to tell that story—that simple, chronological story—on Friday night put a lump in my throat as hard as a fist. What I wanted more than anything else, I realized, was for things to go on the way they were forever.

I hadn't talked to anyone but my family that week, and I wondered how many people in town even knew I was back. A couple of friends from high school had called, but I had asked my mother to tell them I wasn't home and she had nodded and returned to the phone and said, "He's out right now. Can he call you back?" in a friendly sing-song way. And it struck me then—or maybe it was later, much later, I can't really be sure—but it struck me that if I had been at the other end of that phone, I would have believed her. She was that convincing.

"Why don't they mind their own business?" my father said. "They always call during dinner. They're worse than salespeople. They want more from you than salespeople." He called them busy bodies. He called them vampires and ghouls.

"It's just interest," my mother said. "Interest and concern."

While I was away, she had written me long letters about people in the neighborhood—who had done what to their homes and what trips they had taken during their summer vacations. She told me that Tim and my father said hello, and that I should take care of myself.

Tim said she wrote these letters early in the morning and left them for the mailman, attached to the mailbox with a clothespin. "It seemed like she was being secretive about it," he said. "Even though I knew she was probably just writing you about the weather. I said to myself, 'What the hell is she telling him?'"

"Nothing much," I said. I had never written her back, but I had read those letters over and over, returning them to their envelopes when I was finished. I think it was as important for my mom to write them as it was for my father to sit down with his two sons and eat a meal he had prepared.

My mother has her story, but many things happened that Friday night that are important enough to remember, to tell. I remember sitting in my father's recliner listening to the television with my eyes closed. As I moved in and out of sleep it seemed that a great deal of time was passing—the characters on the TV changed, the windows darkened—but that was fine with me, I could let the whole evening pass that way. Finally my father roused me by asking if there was anything special I wanted for dinner. I told him, "No, not really," and then, when I realized what time it was, I headed upstairs and knocked lightly on Tim's door. "It's me," I said.

He was sitting on the bed holding a small green lizard. It crawled around his thumb and fingers as he turned his hand over. He dropped it into a shoebox on his windowsill and said, "Hi."

"Where did you get the chameleon?" I asked.

"It's not a chameleon. It's a just a lizard," he said. "I traded something for it."

His walls were bare except for a couple of horror movie posters I had given him when I had been working at the local movie theater. He was bare-chested, and a thin scar stretched from just beneath his nipple down to his stomach. I sat down at the foot of the bed and said, "Are you having dinner with us tonight?"

"I guess," he said. He tapped the side of the shoebox.

I noticed he was holding a sleek yellow all-weather radio, the headphones collar-tight around his neck. I had never noticed it before and I guessed that it would be gone in a few days. Objects entered and vanished from Tim's life like that—the leather jacket was nowhere in his room, although there was a camera with a zoom lens on his dresser and a shoebox full of painted seashells and junk jewelry on the floor.

"Do you remember that game we used to play when we were kids?" he asked.

"What game?"

"The one in the woods behind the school."

"Oh," I said.

"What?"

"I don't know. I just hadn't thought about it in a long time."

The game was like hide-and-seek only rougher. One person hid while the rest hunted him down. When they found him they dragged him back to whatever base camp had been established earlier. The person to evade capture longest—by finding a good hiding place, by kicking and twisting and punching when that hiding place had been found out—that person won. "It was a dumb game," I said, remembering the times I had twisted Tim's arm behind his back or grabbed him in a headlock. I had been good at it.

"It was okay," Tim said. "It was kind of fun," and I wondered why he would think such a thing.

My father yelled from the kitchen. He needed the pepper maybe, or more eggs, or butter when all we had was margarine. From the

100

tone of his voice I got the impression that he thought my mother deliberately hid these things from him.

"Hey," he yelled up to us. "I need somebody to go to the store and get me some mushrooms. Tim. Tim, where are you?"

"In my room," Tim yelled back. "Can't Scott go?"

"I want *you* to go," my father yelled.

"All right. All right."

Bare-chested like that, dressed in nothing but some cut-off jeans, he looked even thinner. He pulled a T-shirt on and said, "Hey, why don't you come along?" He smiled and I knew that he had *something* planned. I remembered what I used to do in high school—the slow drives around and around the center of town, as if we were searching for something—and decided that this was much better than what my father had in mind for us.

In the driveway, Tim offered me the keys, and we stood there for a moment, listening to the bug light crackle from across the street. I hadn't driven the entire week I had been back, and the idea of doing it then, in the dark with Tim next to me, put a knot in my stomach.

"That's okay, no thanks," I said, which I think disappointed him. Before he had his license, I used to drive him all over town, scaring him a little at stop signs when I tapped the break lightly and then gunned the car through the intersection and up the wide, empty street.

"You watch a lot of television," he said, after we had been driving a while.

"Yeah," I said. I looked down at my hands. The way he drove surprised me. He was slow and careful, almost timid, as if he thought something was going to jump out at him from the sidewalk. A large cross dangled from his ear, and I wondered if this was a sign of popularity, or if it marked him as an outcast. His free hand touched it

101

occasionally, eyes never wavering from the road. "I don't put it in that often," he said. "Otherwise, my ear gets infected."

"We should probably get back," I said.

"In a minute," he said. "I want to show you something."

I opened the glove compartment and found a row of tapes by bands I had never heard of, song titles containing words like *death* and *blood*. I turned one of the tapes over in my hand. "They're from Brazil," he said. "The guitarist killed himself with a shotgun. All sorts of good bands are coming out of Brazil, because the conditions down there are so bad." He looked at me then and said, "I'm sorry. Maybe I shouldn't have said that." Then he grinned the way he had at the house that morning. "Maybe it doesn't matter. I don't know."

"So Dad doesn't care if you listen to heavy metal music?" I said. He probably noticed me trying to shift the subject over just a little, but my guess is he didn't care.

He said, "It's called death metal."

"Well," I said. "That's completely different," and his smile widened, breaking out into laughter. It was loud and unashamed and nice to hear. The road moved past a municipal park and then narrowed as the houses thinned out. Tim frowned and wiped the back of his hand across his nose. He seemed to be remembering something.

"Hey, tell me about the army," he said, and then he made a nervous gesture, a kind of half-grab at the air, as if he were swatting a fly. "I mean, if you don't want to talk about it, that's fine."

"I don't mind," I said. "I don't *think* I do." We turned onto a side road and he clicked the high beams on. There were a lot of trees, lawns, the occasional expensive-looking house set far back from the road. I said, "I thought I was escaping, you know, but it turned out I wasn't."

I remembered the argument with my father that summer when I told him what I was going to do, the satisfaction that came with knowing he was powerless to stop me. I wondered what kind of escape Tim had mapped out in his imagination. He was in his senior year and I hadn't heard him talk about any plans.

"Dad says you were in over your head," Tim said. "He says he knew you were heading into trouble." I didn't say anything. What could I say? Tim smiled and added, almost as an afterthought, "Of course, Mom doesn't talk about it too much. The only thing she's really said is that she thinks you did the best you could under the circumstances. Can you believe that? The best you could under the circumstances."

I wondered exactly what my mother meant by that. In its way, it was a good story, one in which I had arrived here back at home as a result of effort and decision on my part. Maybe she had thought I had simply found a loophole and used it. And maybe that was true. I wanted to believe it myself.

"What are you going to do now?" Tim asked.

"I'm not sure," I said. "I'm waiting to see what's going to happen."

"Fair enough," he said.

"We really should head back," I said. "They're going to wonder where we went."

"They can wait a little while," he said.

We took a left onto what I thought was another road, but when I saw the single house at the end, I realized it was a long driveway. I thought of the house parties I used to go to, but there were no cars there, nothing to indicate a party of any kind.

Tim turned off the headlights and slowed down to a crawl. I could hear the gravel popping under the tires as he pulled to a stop. He said, "Let's walk the rest of the way," and I followed him up to the house.

There was a light on in the upstairs window and I began to dread what was going to happen next, because I thought I had figured it out, that I could see how the next few minutes might unfold—the door opening and a rich kid with a stoned look in his eyes saying hello, the exchange of money for whatever he was selling, and the offer from Tim to smoke it in the car while we headed back to dinner. But even as I was thinking it, that did not seem right. It was a beautiful house and I could imagine the kind of person who would live in such a place. She was probably upstairs right now, in her oversized bedroom, talking on the phone to a friend who lived in a similar bedroom in a similar house. It filled me with a familiar melancholy feeling, just thinking about her. She was warm and sheltered and she thought she was happy. Maybe Tim had a love-hate relationship with her and he was planning some kind of practical joke.

The truth was, I admitted, I didn't know what was happening, and I wanted to find out more than I wanted to stop it. I followed Tim around back, where he lifted the welcome mat and shook it out, then started rummaging around in the plants to one side of the door, lifting fistfuls up wood chips and dropping them. Finally, after what seemed like a long time, he reached up and ran his hand along the top of the door. "Damn it," he said, but there wasn't really any anger in his voice. He took a putty knife from his back pocket and jammed it into the window frame and pried the window loose. Then he reached inside and opened the door. "Come on," he said.

There were dishes on the countertop and in the sink. A plate smeared with catsup and a small pile of cold French Fries. A glass with orange juice pulp clinging to the inside. It was as if we had interrupted an intimate moment. Tim opened the refrigerator and stood there, slouched, inspecting the contents. "I'm hungry," he said. "Do you want anything?"

I hung back in the doorway. "What are you doing?"

"I'm just looking around," he said. Suddenly it was as if he realized he still held the putty knife in his hand. I recognized the paint-spattered green handle from the tool rack in our father's garage. Tim slipped it back in his pocket, then opened the freezer. He took out a Popsicle and began to unwrap it.

"Don't worry," he said. They're gone for the weekend."

He dropped the wrapper on the floor, put the Popsicle in his mouth, decided he didn't want it, and threw it underhand in the general direction of the trash. Then he looked at me and fake-scowled, his lips curled back from his teeth in a dog snarl. For a second he looked like he was going to charge me and I wondered what I'd do if he did.

"Oh, don't give me that look," he said, and he grinned. "You're no angel. I know your record."

"I threw some rocks at some windows," I said, which was not the whole truth. It was enough to make him laugh again, although this time the laugh seemed forced. It struck me then that everything he was doing seemed a little forced. He was showing off for me. He walked into the other room.

"Look at this," he said, when he walked into the next room. He had a glass ball in his hand. It was about the size of a softball and it seemed to be made of wafer-thin interlocking plates. He faked a throw to me and I jumped a little, hands out, ready to catch it, but he was already holding it up to the track lighting, watching the reflections on its surface. He said, "I wonder what it's for?"

"Just to look at, I think," I said.

He chuckled. "People make me sick."

He walked into the next room, still carrying the ball, and I lingered behind, looking at the books lined up on the bookcase. Someone had taken the time to put them in alphabetical order. I took one of the books out, felt its weight in my hand in the same way Tim had felt the weight of the glass globe. I flipped through the pages without reading them.

"Everything feels better when you do it in someone else's house," Tim said, when I entered the other room. He was sitting, hunched forward in a rocking chair. "Food tastes better. You should have something to eat." I realized then that I still held the book in my hand and I set it on the couch. It felt satisfying, somehow, to have disrupted the order of the bookcase a little.

"We should go," I said.

"In a little while. I have to look upstairs."

"How often have you done this?"

"A few times." He smiled and ran a hand through his hair. "It's a phase I'm going through." Although he was gangly he had a nice face, sunken cheeks, the large eyes of someone you could trust. He would be handsome in a few years. I could easily picture someone falling in love with him. I could picture him hurting that person in the same off-handed way he had jimmied the door to this house and slipped inside.

"How many people do you think live here?" I asked.

"No kids. It's too neat." He looked hard at me. "It's a little thrill, that's all. I thought you'd get a kick out of it. I really did. Remember that time you put an M-80 in the high school toilet?" He smiled. "That's like, almost a stick of dynamite, isn't it?"

"I thought we were going to egg the place or something."

"Did you see any eggs? Why would you think that? Anyway, Dad would kill me. He needs all the eggs to make those weird omelets." His voice rose to a light trill. "He needs to *feed* us."

I said, "I'm worried about you."

He seemed to think about that for a second and then he said, "You should be worried about yourself. I'm not saying that to be mean or anything, but compared to you, I'm doing fine."

He laughed then because he realized where we were, I think, what he was saying. And then he reached over and picked up the globe from the coffee table. The kind of family who would own such a thing would be just the kind of family that Tim would despise.

"It bothers me sometimes," he said. "You used to be so together. I looked up to you. I mean, I *still* look up to you."

"I used to knock you around," I said. "That's what I used to do."

He grimaced and looked down at the ornament in his hand. "We were playing games," he said, "and anyway, you didn't mean it," and then he shifted the ball from hand to hand. He glanced over at a picture on the bookcase—a father and mother and two children and an older woman who was probably the grandmother. "They have kids after all," he said, as he scanned the floor. "But where are the toys? Neatly tucked away in the closets?" He moved over to the photograph and tilted his head, as if studying it, but his eyes were watching me. "What a happy bunch of people. The father looks so pleasant, doesn't he? He looks extremely *pleasant*."

I was reminded of something our father had said when we had been arguing about my decision to join up. "I might not be the most *pleasant* person in the world," he said, "but I'm one of the few people who is going to look after you. That's the truth." Tim had been standing there as we talked.

I picked up the book again. My hands needed something to do.

Tim said, "I'll tell you why I think you watch all that television. You like to be part of the background. That's what watching all that television does to you. You can hide in plain sight, right at the center of the house. I've seen it. We just walk around you like you're hardly there and you can listen to everything and make notes in your head."

"That's an interesting theory," I said.

He said, "Can I see your wrists?"

Maybe he was figuring out a new way to admire me. Maybe he thought that what I had done would make us closer than we had ever been. The question didn't catch me by surprise. It seemed to be the logical extension of the trip, the talk we were having. Maybe it was his way of saying, I've been honest with you, now you be honest with me.

I said, "You've got to be kidding. Let's go."

"I just want to see," he said.

"No."

"It puts it all in perspective," he said, and he looked around the room with contempt. "I mean, what is all this? I don't care about things. Nobody owns anything anyway, not really."

"That's a convenient thing for a thief to believe, Tim," I said, and he flinched a little, and I realized that he was trying to be sincere, trying to share something important with me.

It suddenly seemed that anything I said now might harm him, because in bringing me here he had knowingly placed himself in my hands. I thought about hurting him—this word, that word—

and I didn't know if I wanted that or not, didn't know if that's what he needed.

"Hey, I'm not the only one standing here," he said.

Maybe I should have. Maybe I should have tried harder to hurt him. But my voice was quiet and patient. "On the way here I said I didn't know what I was going to do. What about you? Do you know what you're going to do?"

He laughed for the third or fourth time that night.

"Sure. I have it all figured out. I'm going to move to Canada and find a little piece of land to squat on. I'll build a cabin. I'll grow a beard." I couldn't tell if he was joking or not. He said, "I'm going to graduate, if that's what you mean," and then he stood up. "I have to scrounge upstairs." And then he bent down so that his hand was almost touching the floor and he dropped the globe. It made a hard clunking sound, but it didn't break.

I sat there and listened to drawers opening and closing from the bedrooms, and I found myself thinking about lying in my cot in the morning. I would always wake early and lie motionless in bed for ten minutes, waiting for the day to catch up with me, for people to spill out of their cots, the drills, breakfast. Those were the best moments of the day, lying there, because I was not *part* of the day yet. I was outside looking in, looking ahead. It occurred to me then that those moments had now expanded to fill just about my entire life, which had become flat and beautiful in its simplicity. Even sitting there, on someone else's couch in someone else's house, it felt as if I were *not really* there, the way a ghost must feel. Maybe it was something like what Tim felt whenever he climbed through a window or jimmied a door. I knew he didn't steal much from the houses he robbed. There was something else he was after.

I could picture what was happening at our home. The table had been set and unset, the food cooked and then packed away. Our father had paced the house at first. He had yelled and threatened to head out and prowl around town looking for us. Meanwhile, this other family—this nameless, perfect family—was on vacation somewhere, completely unaware of what was happening in their own home. Did our father have any idea? Was he attentive to what we had become and his part in it?

I looked at the globe. I wanted to pick it up and put it on the original bookshelf, but maybe one shelf down, a little more to the right. A little mystery for the returning family. Tim came back into the room and I unbuttoned the sleeves of my shirt and held out my hands. "Here," I said. "Look."

"Why?" he asked.

I wanted that smile to vanish. If it had been two years before, I would have hit him—I would have stood up and struck him hard in the mouth—but instead I said, "It's simple, Tim—because I wanted to kill myself."

He pursed his lips. "No," he said. "That's not true. You might think it's true, but it's not. I know why you did it."

And he was right. He was right and I was wrong. I didn't know it then, but I would know it soon.

I almost didn't hear the sound. A car was coming, maybe two cars, from the sound of it. "This way," Tim said. He was heading toward the cellar door, and he was calm, as if this kind of thing had happened to him before. "I think there was a bulkhead," he said. "We can go out there." But I stayed where I was. Running seemed to be the most ridiculous thing in the world to do right then.

"Come on," he said, and I could hear the back door opening,

which was enough to push me into motion, down the stairs, out through the bulkhead, halfway across the freshly cut lawn. There was a police car in the driveway, a flashlight panning across the house. It touched me and I froze.

Tim kept running. He was almost to the woods, but he either thought about me or thought about his car and he stopped and turned around, hands above his head in a half-sarcastic defeated gesture.

He wanted to appear confident and uncaring, I think, but to me he looked frightened and confused. He was smart enough to know that this moment would probably come eventually and most likely he was already past it. In his mind the handcuffing and the ride in the patrol car were already over. He was looking ahead to our father, in bed, reaching across our mother for the phone.

The last time I talked to Tim was almost four years ago. He called just to say hello, he said, although I had not talked to him for more than a year and it was late, late enough that when the phone first rang I thought that something awful had happened. I was surprised to hear Tim's voice saying, "Hey, how are you?" and more surprised that the call came from Chicago. My mother had told me she didn't know where he was and I had imagined him someplace more exotic. He *was* in some kind of trouble, I could tell, although he was joking with me, and I thought, how strange that time has passed and that we're talking in this way.

"Tell me something, Scott," he said. "When did I become the bad son? Can you tell me that?"

When I remember Tim standing there, in someone else's yard, hands above his head, I remember seeing fear in his face, but of course I can't be sure about that. It was night, after all, and the light was shining on me, on my face, not Tim's. And I know *I* was afraid, but more than afraid. I felt pride in having been exposed, in saying, *this is who we are. We are together in this, if only in this single moment.* I wonder if Tim felt that too.

Maybe Tim didn't mind getting caught, not really, not when he would be able to see the effect it would have on our father. I know there are all sorts of ways to punish someone. The cuts on my wrists must have hurt our father much more than they hurt me.

The night had almost turned into morning by the time my father picked us up. None of us talked as he drove us home. I read the billboards as they passed and waited for him or Tim to say something.

"Those damned police," he finally said. "They can't even treat a person with dignity. I went to high school with a couple of those idiots, and I know the only reason they ended up as cops is that they were familiar with the *other* side of the justice system. He who is without sin cast the first stone, that's what I say."

The skyline was gray and smudged and it was easy to believe that we could keep on this way forever, but I was sitting in back and I think this gave me enough strength to finally say something, although I don't remember what it was. Maybe a comment about the weather.

I remember exactly what my father said in reply. "I've been worried to death," he said, in a clipped way that made it an accusation. This was something he had stored up in his head, I could tell, edited, refined. He wasn't just talking about what happened that night. Then he said, "I've tried, you know. I've tried very hard with both of you. And I thought that maybe we were getting somewhere. I really did. But this." He clicked the windshield wipers on low then, because it was starting to drizzle, and when it must have become clear that Tim and I weren't going to say anything—couldn't say anything—he went on. "Your mother doesn't know. I don't know what I'm going to tell her. What do you think I should tell her, Tim? What would you say?"

"I don't know," Tim said. "Tell her the truth. Tell her that her kids are a mess. That's a starting place. You can go on from there." My father raised his hand, as if to slap him. Then—just when I thought he wasn't going to—he did. He reached out and, without really looking, knocked Tim across the jaw. The car wavered in its lane and then we slowed for the exit. It was almost as if it hadn't happened at all.

We took a right at the intersection, onto a road that would lead us outside of town. Maybe he wasn't paying attention. Maybe he needed time to consider what had just happened.

For a second I thought of saying, "Dad, I think we should have gone straight back there," but I didn't. I didn't do anything. We turned onto a narrow road that I knew lead to more narrow roads. "I'm sorry about that," our father said, "but I'm trying to talk to you, you know. And all you can give me is attitude."

"I wasn't trying to give you attitude," Tim said.

"Yes," he said. "Yes, you were. You were *blaming* me."

"I wasn't," Tim said. He was running his hand over his cheek, checking carefully for marks. "Hey," he said. "Where are we going?"

"God damn it," my father said. "Listen. Just listen for a second."

But he had nothing else to say. He was flexing his hands on the steering wheel and glancing from side to side, but somehow his anger didn't seem genuine. Maybe he had felt this way so many times, about so many things, that he couldn't help but go through the motions.

"It's all of them," he finally said, with a wave of his hand and a look out the window. He seemed to be staring down all the people who had ever done him wrong, the people he had just left behind

113

and the people who would be calling the house in the next few days, trying to break into the suspended bubble of our lives—everyone except for the three of us. I followed the gesture outside, to the unfamiliar road, the trees sliding by, and I realized then that I didn't know where we were.

When I talk to my mother about that car ride the story comes out stilted and half-formed. It isn't *really* what I want to say, but I *don't know* what I want to say, so I keep talking. She listens carefully, as if she can see past the noise I'm making to the story that eludes me, and then she smiles in a way that seems rueful and resigned. "Those were difficult times," she says, and there is an awkward silence while we wait for her to continue. There are three of us at the table this time, her, her boyfriend, and me.

She is too old to marry again, she says sometimes, although she loves this man. He is a retired plumber who likes to tell jokes and stories about all the things he saw while fixing people's sinks and toilets. When he is not telling stories he is quiet and what my mother calls even-keeled, and although I don't know him well, I like him.

We are almost always in a restaurant when my mother begins to talk like this, and it is late and we are drinking a little, because I don't see her often and when I do we like to celebrate. She stares over at me, studies me, then back over at her boyfriend. "He had a very difficult time growing up," she says, "and now look at him. Successful. Happy."

And he does—he looks at me—and grins in apology, because he knows I don't like this attention. I can't help but wonder about how he sees us, the three of us, years ago in that car—Tim, who is in Chicago; me, sitting across from him; and my father, who still lives in the same town, the same house, although I don't speak to him much anymore, and when I do, we don't talk about the time we spent under that roof together.

"Yeah, well," he says. "You can't judge a book." And then we both wait for her to finish up what I've started. It can be funny or maudlin or inspiring, depending on her mood and ours.

She usually begins by talking about what she was doing when we arrived home. It was early morning and she was making a cake, a pie, something like that. My father was out somewhere and the kitchen was empty and she wanted to make use of the time. It felt good to her, she says, sneaking in like that when he wasn't around.

"Scott looked awful," she adds. "He looked so tired." And she glances in my direction again. For a second I think she wants me to say something, but then she goes on.

"That was the turning point," she says. "If there was one that was it. He started to pull himself together again after that. I knew he would shake it off. He was just depressed. It wasn't like he had *planned* to go out there with Tim."

Stories, like people, are fragile things. Sometimes we think we have such a firm grip on them that we *possess* them, but they can slip away from us. My mother speaks about that time casually, but carefully, because I think she is trying hard to hold onto it.

The story she tells is about me, about the difficult time in my life that has receded safely into the distant past. It is about her too, in the same way—two people who happened to have a little grace and perseverance and luck. It's important to make this understood, to her boyfriend, and to me, and maybe to herself.

She doesn't mention my father except in the most perfunctory way, partially in deference to this new relationship, I think, possibly as a politeness to me. Tim is then what he is now—his father's son, a product of his work and anger and misguided love. When she's finished it's her boyfriend's turn to tell one of his stories. They are short and have punch lines that never fail to make me chuckle and I'm thinking wait, because my mother's story isn't really finished. There is more to say.

I think my father saw himself, his family, hanging between one life and another, and if he couldn't revisit that old life, maybe he had decided that he could at least delay entering that new life as long as he could. There are many times like that, I know now, when it feels as if you have jumped but not landed yet, and that you don't want to land, not ever, not if you can help it. They last for a second or a night or a few weeks and sometimes even years.

He was driving, that was all. He had no destination in mind, except that he knew that he didn't want to go home and repeat the story of that evening to my mother. He had both hands on the wheel and he was leaning forward and he looked older then—narrow-eyed, quiet, staring out into the dark.

I can remember exactly what my father said when he slowed down and glanced up at me in the rearview mirror, and *this* is what I want to tell my mother, sitting there talking in that restaurant—that he rocked back and forth in his seat slightly, as if to jog himself awake, and said, "I'm tired."

"Me too," Tim said. His eyes were closed, head back, as if he were concentrating on something, as if he were dreaming and listening at the same time.

We had stopped in the middle of the road. It was almost morning. I climbed out of the car and opened the door for my father. He got out and then Tim got out and they stood and watched me while I opened the trunk and removed a frayed blanket. It was an old blanket—I remembered it from when I first started to drive that car—and it felt good to find it still there next to the jack and the jumper cables and all the other things someone might need if they were ever in trouble.

"Here," I said, and I placed it on the seat like a pillow, and our father got in back and I got in front and I turned us slowly around and tried to remember the way we had come.

DEAR

THOSE OLD MYSTERY STORIES ALWAYS BEGIN with the clatter of weather so I will remind you of the rain that night, tumbling down hard on my roof and across your windshield as you headed home.

It was past midnight when you finally called, and the first words out of your mouth were, "Nancy was fired and I killed a dog," as if one had led to the other.

"Slow down," I said. "What are you talking about?"

I began to wash my dinner dishes as you talked. If that seems insensitive, then I'm sorry, but you *always* had a dangerous tale to tell about something, and maybe I just needed to do something with my fumbling, hairy hands. You told me you had been drinking at your favorite bar in Cambridge—the one with overstuffed chairs and Guinness on draft—and you had decided to take the back roads home, as a way to avoid the police. Then your voice broke as you told me about the idiot dog, its sad arrogance in thinking it owned that empty street, and the way it lurched into the road like it was the drunken one.

"It was practically suicidal," you said.

As I listened to the dreary tapping on my roof I thought of you following the blurred brake lights of some ghost car off in the middle distance, until you found another beacon, honed in on it, accelerating until you passed that one as well. That's how you would have found

119

your way home. I had driven with you before, of course, the fingers of my right hand resting on the dash.

I pushed a sponge into a wineglass, twisted it around as you said something about the dog's head, so low to the ground, as if it were eating something—maybe some errant squirrel, victim of another troubled driver.

One plate, two glasses, and a salad bowl. I set them upside down in the dish drainer and watched water collect in small pools beneath them. You said, "I'm having a nervous breakdown."

"Ah," I said, because how can someone reply to that?

The image of your face came to mind, your long roman nose, your steely eyes, and the way you clicked your tongue against the back of your teeth when you were anxious. "I need to come over," you continued. "I need to get out of this house. Nancy's in the other room looking at photographs from New Mexico again, and it's driving me crazy. It's like she's in some kind of fantasy world."

"It's just New Mexico," I said. "New Mexico isn't a fantasy world. It's real. It's one of the United States of America. You lived there for three years."

"Hey," you said. "I know where I've lived."

"The weather there is great," I continued. "There are really good drugs there." I was remembering your stories, giving them back to you.

"Yeah," you said. "Marijuana butter." It was easy to believe that people were ninety-something percent water from the wet sounds you were making in the back of your throat. "I'm really losing it," you said.

"We both are," I said. "We're losing it together." Although I did not feel very bad at all.

"If I wasn't such a coward I'd put a gun to my head and kapow

kapow, you know? Like that guy in the movie we saw last year. What was the name of that movie?"

I said, "We just need to get some sleep."

You said, "I killed a living thing today."

"It's not your fault," I said, not because I knew every intricate circumstance of that night, but because nothing seemed to be anybody's fault. The stove clock was ticking away the time nervously. "What kind of dog was it?" I finally said, because I couldn't think of anything else to drop into the near-silence.

"Golden Retriever," you mumbled.

"They're one of the dumbest breeds," I explained. "They're practically birds. Their bones snap like twigs and they run out into roads all the time. Statistically, they're the number one breed killed by cars. And not by a nose width, either, Michael. By a long margin. A wide margin is what I mean. A wide margin. It's like they were bred for that kind of thing. What did you do?"

You seemed to consider this. "What did I do? I stopped and I rolled down my window and looked at it. I looked at it and then I left."

And then you must have heard something—a click, a secret breath—because you said, "Nancy? Nancy, is that you? Are you on the line? Nancy?"

"It's nobody," I said.

"Nancy," you said. "Hang up the phone right now. God Damn it, Nancy. Hang up."

"Michael," I said. "There's nobody there."

"I'm coming over," you said, "so we can have a *private* conversation. You stay where you are. Put some tea on. I'll be over in twenty minutes."

And this is the strange part. It's the part that, if you told a person, they wouldn't believe you.

Because I turned the burner on under the teapot and watched it steam and listened to it whistle and then poured the water and let the water grow cold as I read the paper and you never came—not that night, and not the next, and not in the month of June, and not in early July, and not in late July, when Nancy needed you most, and not in August, when I expected you to appear as if by magic.

I never spoke to you again, and neither did Nancy, and how strange is that when the last words someone ever says to you are, "I'll be right over?"

These words would make you laugh, but I don't care. I only allow you here as a ghost, a mirror to throw my bad acting against, so I can see the shape of my lips when I make the words, the meanness in my ugly eyes.

It's September now and missing you has become a bad habit, like biting the side of my thumb while reading a novel. I still drive up Route 121, past the horse farms, past the boarded-up Dairy Queen, and I walk that long stretch of beautiful woods, pacing up and down like a prisoner calling your name.

But at the same time I'm free, aren't I? I have begun visiting the narrow little bars in this town, chatting with the person two stools over about whatever is on the television. I make the trip to Maine to visit my family every few weekends. My sister, she says I seem content, and occasionally asks me if I have met someone. "No," I tell her, but I smile like I'm keeping a little secret.

Picture me—gorilla-shouldered, chubby-cheeked little me— standing at the edge of a small stream, hands cupped to my mouth, shouting your name into the trees. We skied through those woods in February, you leading the way, until we came across a long cabin with a burned black roof. It had been painted bright yellow recently, and there was a combination padlock on the door. "What's this?" you said, as you padded around it, but I knew you had discovered it before, had orchestrated the whole trip to have us arrive at that spot. You were always doing things like that.

Your favorite color was yellow.

The tumblers of the lock fell into place, the padlock slipped off the door, and we scrambled inside. You lit a fire in the woodstove as I tugged loose my ski straps. "Those bearded has-beens in my department are trying to force me out," you said. "I have more articles published than any three of them combined and I'm not even forty-five yet. It's jealousy, plain and simple."

You knew how I felt about those bearded old men in their large offices. Sometimes when working late, grading a stack of composition papers, I pushed out my chair, exited my narrow office, and took a walk. Always I found myself at that ivy-covered building, the large one across from the Humanities House, and wandered up and down the wide hall. In the early evening before heading home to Cambridge and Newton these old men with beards left their waste paper baskets outside their locked doors for the janitor to empty, and occasionally I plucked crumpled notes from these gray receptacles—even the trash cans had a kind of battered, aged authority, and I was careful not to upset them too much with my prying hands. I smoothed the notes out against the wall, stole their thoughts with my eyes, although the numbers and scribbles did not make much sense.

Some of that trash, I must admit, was yours. The best of it.

"They resent your suave charm," I said.

"Yes," you said with a smirk. "My suave charm."

We both knew why we were there in that cabin. The floor was covered with squat candles, which you lit with a wand of rolled newspaper. Then you produced a bottle of cheap Merlot from somewhere and corkscrewed off the top. I pulled my shirt off over my head and you fell back into a nest of blankets and pillows. It looked warm there, in the dusty glow from a cracked skylight, but I put up my usual token resistance, said something about the threat of snow. You were lying on your back, kicking off your pants. We could see our breath.

"What's Nancy doing today?" I asked, as another way to put on the brakes. But my body was moving. I was crouching on the floor next to you, and you were passing me the bottle. I waved it away.

"She's probably out taking pictures of dead trees," you said, and you put the bottle to your mouth again, corked it, and moved to kiss me. It was the first time I had heard you talk about her work that way—usually you were so reverential about her photography—but it wasn't the last. I guess I felt that your honesty—that jewel-like glint of snideness—was a gift to me, and I kissed you back.

Your mouth tasted like the wine, of course. You always tasted like liquor—good wines, vanilla vodka, brandy, sometimes cheap beer, depending on your mood. I grew to like that taste—it was like I was sharing just a little bit of your topsy-turvy, self-destructive charisma.

"It'll warm you up," you said, so I took a drink.

"We can't help being thirsty moving toward the voice of water," I said, quoting Rumi.

"Poetry," you said. You smirked like you had just seen an amusing oddity—a child with an obscenely bad haircut, an obese man showing his butt crack. "Beautiful," you said. "But what does it mean? It means nothing." And you twirled yourself around me and then over me.

I wanted to explain, but we had moved onto other things.

Sometimes I would come to the clearing and stand there, listening to my own labored breath and the birds clattering in the trees. The more I looked at that shed with the burned black roof, the more I became convinced that you were buried behind it.

At the same time, I was equally convinced that you had crossed the pine-speckled border into Canada—that you had remarried, grown a generous mane of hippy hair, and given yourself a new surname. I convinced myself that you were thinking of having children, that one of them would bear my name like a secret little joke. "I bet you he's in Vancouver," I told Nancy's answering machine—your answering machine—in mid-March. "He's living it up in Vancouver, Canada. You need to change your greeting by the way. It's a little unsettling. Call me back, okay?"

This is how your wife and I have come to know each other—through these phone calls, and through those five or six dinners, you seated between us, topping off my wine glass and telling your ridiculous stories. You introduced me as your star student, and I felt that buzz that comes from being the pupil singled out by the teacher—this despite the fact that I was a teacher myself, a thirty-six-year-old English instructor, a lover of E.M. Forster, Edith Warton, and Evelyn Waugh.

"I find economics depressing," Nancy said with a smile. "It's like a religion with him."

She made a dismissive gesture in your general direction.

I had seen the sentimental movies about young disciples, the kindly mentors, and sitting around that benevolent table, I tried so hard to say intelligent, charming things. I settled into the lie greedily, as if it were the food placed in front of me. "He's doing important work," I said, thinking of swarms of numbers. Nancy touched the back of my hand and told me I was different than the others— meaning your other students, I suppose, the other young men you had brought into your dining room. So it doesn't seem odd that we might meet for one more meal without you; yet it seems more impossible than your return.

"Hey, Kephalis," she said back to my answering machine, when she returned my call. She is always using my last name, as if she were my gym coach barking at me to do more push-ups. "Vancouver, huh? I was thinking Alberta. Let's have dinner soon."

The loop of your voice still greeted me when I ping-ponged her call back. "Alberta, Vancouver, it's all the same," I said to the machine. "Give me a ring. I'm working late tomorrow though, so call back after seven."

"Do you think he's with somebody?" she said back, when she called at five the next day, her voice softer. "I mean, seriously, I think there was somebody else. Well, she can have him, I don't care. I have an interview next week, by the way."

"Great to hear about the interview," I said in mid-June. "How did it go? Call me back when you get a chance. Dinner would be great."

"I think he's dead," she said, in early July, when they found your truck in the mall parking lot. It couldn't have been later than five in the morning and I could hear her voice from my bed, where I had been sleeping soundly. The sound of that voice was so plaintive—so fragile—that it would have been a violation for me to pick up the receiver and interrupt her, so I rolled over and listened, breathing into my pillow. "Jesus," she said. "I still had the feeling he was just going to appear at the door full of apologies."

You see, I had imagined you back to life so completely that I had begun to think that you might call. And when the phone rang I thought in my dreaminess, Ah, this is it.

And then Nancy's voice instead of yours.

Finally I swung my heavy legs out of bed, pulled on my jeans, my boots, a wrinkled shirt, and headed out to the woods, pushing my way through the pine branches.

Certainly I had *wanted* to pick up the receiver and interrupt her conversation with my machine. I would have opened my mouth and simply let the truth fly out. Then something else would fill that space, I decided, if I should just empty it, something full and satisfying like those long, leisurely meals we used to eat together.

But instead I was trudging my way to our silly little house.

The first thing I noticed upon arriving was that some thorn bushes had been cleared from around back and dragged into a small brush pile. When I cupped my hands around my face and bent to look into the window, I could see the stocky candles, the neatly folded blankets, and something else—a large spider plant, the tips of its leaves brown, hanging from a hook fastened into the ceiling. I certainly would have remembered it, had it been there before, but I did not. It hung around my height, in the center of the room, and I would have been forced to crouch to avoid smacking my forehead against it.

The padlock was securely fastened, the windows unbroken.

I tested the lock—vainly twisting the numbers around and around and listening to the clicks—not because I wanted to enter your sneaky little paradise, but because I wanted to save that plant. Its leaves were turning brown, and although sunlight streamed through the skylight, I was sure the soil in the pot was dry.

And yet breaking the window seemed like heresy. Despite my

trips through the halls of the faculty offices I was not a vandal and I was reminded by the mystery of this hanging plant that I had only been a visitor in this place.

Back at the car, I noticed other tire tracks, in a place where few if any people would ever park. I wondered if hunters ever came here, or young couples with their animals, and if they had claimed the place as their own. Did a different padlock hang on the door? The idea of two other people making love there seemed to me one of those casual cruelties life offered up from time to time as an object lesson. It made me want to become the vandal I had been so sure I couldn't be—to smash the window with my shirt-wrapped hand.

The skylight would be the best way to enter—or at least the most dramatic—but I was due at work soon, and I was hungry, and I didn't know if I had it in me anyway—to enter that place like a cat burglar. So I went to work, where I moved from office to office, until I came to yours. I let myself in, looked through your files, your desk, your neatly sharpened pencils. When you had first gone missing I spirited away the Jim Beam from the bottom of your desk, so that nobody would find it, but as I sat in your chair I wished I had not been so fastidious, so I could lean back and take a long swig from the bottle, close my eyes, and feel as reckless as you. Did you ever want to feel like me?

That night, a message for me. Nancy, of course, saying, "If I don't find work soon I'm going to start selling his stuff."

During an idle moment at the college I dropped your name into the search engine on a library computer, and you came back to me in fragments, an article here, an article there, the titles as long and incomprehensible as centipedes. It seemed incredible that you wrote such things about the Federal Reserve Bank while living the life of a sad little rock-and-roll star. As I scanned the articles, a student came up behind me, said hello quietly, his hand on the edge of the table.

I glanced up and around. I recognized him from the open lecture you had given more than a year before—he wore the same Oakland A's baseball cap, turned backward on his head, although he had grown a peach-fuzz moustache. I remembered him standing in the back, raising his hand tentatively. He had asked you a question and you had chuckled and thrown a few sentences his way, like bones to a dog. I had asked the question after that—somehow his failure had made me brave—and you said, "Now that's a question!" and called me by name even though we had never spoken. Then you asked me something back—something glib about the critical thinking abilities of the average TV-suckled eighteen-year-old—as if we were having a private conversation in front of two hundred people. "Let's continue this some other time," you joked, and that was that.

"He doesn't teach here anymore," I said over my shoulder, as the names of the articles scrolled by.

The boy, he was looking at the computer screen, at your life's work, with a dismissive curl to his lip, as if he had caught me searching for pornography. "Good," he said. "Did they fire his ass?"

I felt my jaw muscles tense to defend you. I was ready to parrot back words you had said about your deep, deep talents and the rigid norms of our society, but he quickly added, "I couldn't believe the way he treated you that day. It was so condescending."

"What day?" I asked.

"Never mind," he said. "Can I have the computer when you're done?"

"You can have it now," I said, because it was time for me to leave anyway.

After my last walk through the woods, I had pledged that I would not return, but you are a hard person to forget, and hearing that boy talk about the past squeezed the days together, so that finding you seemed a simple matter of taking a few steps backward. I did not believe this, of course, but I felt it in the parts of my head and heart that are beyond reason; I felt it even more strongly as I took my bolt cutters from the trunk and headed off down the overgrown path, and even *more* strongly as I dropped them onto the ground, cupped my hands around my face, bent down, peering through the cabin window.

The plant looked worse off, although I couldn't be sure. I imagined it slowly dying as I watched it week after week after week from my side of the glass, and as I watched it, a story came to mind. Not even a story, just a memory, something you probably forgot the day after it happened. Do you remember that rented room in Concord, the diner we ate in the next morning? "Let's get out of here," you had said, as you sucked down the last of your coffee. I thought you were talking about the diner itself, and so I reached for my wallet, but that's not what you meant at all, and you laughed like I was a little kid doing something cute and ridiculous. "Wisconsin," you said. "That would be a great place to live."

What would have happened if I had said yes, stood up, slapped my hands against the edge of the table, and said that I would drive the first five hours? Would you have shrunken back, looked at me as if I were crazy, or would you have smiled and handed me the keys? I was still thinking of that day—and my lack of ambition in imagining our escape—as I smooshed my face against the glass. I had half-expected the plant to be gone, like some mirage that had visited me one time and one time only, but there it was. And not only that, but there were new things there as well—a jumble of blankets, a heavy industrial flashlight, a book folded open on the floor. It was an autobiography of Miles Davis. I could see his familiar wizened pharaoh face splashed across the front. You had lent that book to me once, along with two of his albums, so I am sure you can understand how I was feeling.

I sat down on the ground and dug my fingers into the tall grass. "Get up, you big baby," I expected to hear you say from over my shoulder, from back somewhere in the trees. I looked up then, off into the woods. Nothing but the pines and the patch of earth where thorn bushes had been. That's when I noticed. The earth had been turned up and laid down again, by a spade or shovel. It had been that way before, but I hadn't noticed because I had been so focused on the cabin. Rising to my feet, I looked more closely at the spot. The rocks were muddy with reddish dirt, as if they had been unearthed from deeper in the soil. A single larger stone, the size of a football, had been placed dead center in the bare patch. I walked over, bent down and smoothed my hands over it, then gripped it tightly, preparing to underhand it into the bushes.

And still I expected your voice.

You would have made a joke about my dirty fingers, the resolute set to my jaw, and that ludicrous rock clenched in my hands. And I would have spun around and maybe we both would have laughed then, because even after everything that had happened it would have seemed like a joke. It would have still been easy to forgive.

I tossed the rock and it rolled some distance away, but not nearly as far as I thought it would carry. The force of the throw brought me forward too, down to one knee, right palm against the ground.

And even more surprises, because there *was* a voice, but not yours.

131

A calm, low voice, a man, from behind me, saying, "What are you doing here?" I turned and looked up from my spot on the ground, feeling like I should spin and bolt. "It's me," I said. I don't know why I would say that, except that it was the only truth I knew at that moment. He was young, in his mid-twenties probably, with black hair cut close to his head and thin eyes. Handsome eyes, I decided. We stood assessing each other, and the strangest thoughts occurred to me, a rough sequence of rushed, violent events—my helpless resistance, my yells and kicking, those handsome eyes searching through my wallet, hands sliding over my body, pulling away my clothes, and then the two of us, you and I, buried in the same ground. It was like something conjured up from a gothic romance, and its beauty was as blinding as the sun behind this unknown person who had, while I was lost in reverie, stepped two steps closer. He was lean and tall and dressed in a bright orange crewneck sweater unzipped down the front to reveal a neat yellow pocket-T. God knows why, but the fact that he was a beautiful boy with a serious frown, in expensive, yuppie clothes, made him seem more dangerous.

The pieces fit, at least to me, in that sparking, ridiculous moment when he said your name. "You knew Michael," he said.

"Yes," I said. He did not move; neither did I.

I thought of the heavy bolt cutters behind him, twenty steps from where I stood. He was not holding anything, not even a stick. His hands were not even shaped into fists.

"I expected you to look different," he said. "Younger."

"Yes," I said again. He stood directly in front of me, his arms slack and legs slightly bent in a mirror image of my pose. If he were to step just a little to the right or to the left, then I would be able to move, take those twenty steps, but he didn't move except to open and close his hand, and so I didn't either.

He laughed at my silly answers. It was like you laughing.

In my mind's eye, his hands became less threatening, although they were still moving over your body, tugging at your clothes in a way not unlike the way I had imagined him tugging at mine, unclasping your belt and pulling at your socks. Maybe that was more threatening. I imagined him biting at your mouth.

"He never told me about you," I said. "I'm at a disadvantage."

"You're all he talked about," he said with a slight smile, "but he took ten years off you and thirty pounds."

I was moving now, stepping past him, over to my unused tools. I scissored them open and closed theatrically, as if I were snipping an invisible thread. I wanted him to see the lengths to which I was prepared to go. "I guess I don't need these anymore," I said, "since you must know the combination?"

Once we were inside, he picked up the book—the book you had loaned him—and, holding it open with his thumb, glanced at some hidden sentence, smiling sadly. "Where is he?" I asked, as I stood in the doorway.

"I don't know," he said, and he closed the book. For the first time I noticed how thin he was, and I was ashamed of myself for imagining that this person could hurt me, even if he had tried. Had I wanted to die? I spit the thought away.

"Maybe he's in Wisconsin," I said. I was half-joking, half-serious. I wanted to be the one who knew.

He was passing the combination lock back and forth between his hands. I sat down on a milk crate, the bolt cutters across my knees.

"You are not at all what I expected," he said, screwing the insult just a little deeper. But it felt good to be that surprising and elusive.

"Yes, yes," I said. "He was a liar."

"God," he said. "One of the biggest." He tilted his head back, as if he were speaking to someone up above our heads.

"You were one of his graduate students?" I asked.

"No," he said. "I don't think he ever fucked his students."

"I think he did, actually," I said.

"Yeah, well," he said. "Whatever."

"So who are you?"

"A nobody," he said. "A loser." He tossed the lock up in the air with his right hand and caught it with his left. He was smiling. And I thought of him tossing the lock again, to me this time, underhanded, as if we were friends tossing a softball back and forth. He would fall back onto the blankets and tell me more about you. Then I would do the same. I would tell him about your slow-boil temper, your disgust with a world that didn't move at your breakneck speed, the way you spattered your French fries with catsup and then ate them with a fork. And we would measure our two experiences—which in fact were the same thing—against each other, like kids talking earnestly about the same movie.

Then I would set the lock on the ground—the bolt cutters too—and slide off the crate into a kneeling position, slowly, as if I were trying hard not to startle him. Maybe it would be a way of touching you again—to know you through him—or maybe it would be a small revenge against you, but I would rest my hand on his arm and smooth the blond hairs up to his tense bicep. This is something you used to do to me—I am sure you remember—and I would watch him for some sign that he recognized the gesture. "I was always jealous of you," he would say. "And now here you are."

Our lips would not meet. We would not even fully undress, and at some point, as our bodies pushed up against each other, I would look down and see our ridiculous stocking feet—mine white, his black—and realize that this was another mistake.

When we were done, I would roll to one side so as not to bother him with my body.

"Don't touch me," he said, because I had moved toward him, propelled by the beautiful clockwork mechanism of my fantasy. He scrambled away quickly enough that his shoulder bumped the hanging plant and sent it rocking back and forth. I steadied it with both my hands.

"You're scared of me," I told him.

And for a second I imagined myself through his eyes as someone a little more dangerous, a little stronger. And then I knew what I was looking for—not the complete idea of you, but the complete idea of myself. And at that moment, as your old lover walked past me to the door, this second knot of my own character seemed the more difficult one to untangle. And even then—before I heard what I heard next—I knew it was my vanity and sentimentality driving me forward. You would not have allowed yourself something as middle class as self-knowledge.

"No," he said. "You're just old. And too fat. You're old and fat." He underhanded me the lock, and my imagination intersected with reality for a split second, then arced away again. "It's yours now," he said. "Burn it to the ground for all I care."

I am an articulate person—you have said so yourself, that I have my moments—but I am struck dumb by feeling, and so my mouth fumbled for words. "Wait," was all I managed to say, before he strode off. I could hear his footsteps move down the length of the cabin and then off down the path, crunching branches and leaves. I settled back onto the blankets and let the sunlight drain down through the skylight onto my face.

Long after he had gone, I walked around behind the cabin and began to dig with my hands, pulling back the earth. I was not used to this kind of work, but there was something meditative about it. I had never worked in a garden, but I imagined it might be like this.

Just a little more than a foot down: long hair the color of gold.

Then something tattered and thin, like a torn jacket or rag. I pushed and scraped at it and found something smooth and sharp and white—a tooth. I ran the side of my hand along the ground and revealed more fangs, an open mouth filled with dirt, a dried black nose. The tattered thing, the piece of rag, it was the dog's ear. I uncovered its face, then its neck, and the orange reflective collar and dog tags that probably held a name and address. There were people at that address who had not seen this animal in four months. They slipped into my life for a moment, as pale shadows of my imagination, the way the nameless young man had the hour before as we faced each other in the cabin—the way you had too, I suppose. "Poor thing," I said, marveling at the intricacy of your character.

I left the dog as you left it, returned home, padded my muddy feet across my carpet, registered the blinking light, lifted the receiver, dialed her number—your number—and heard the ridiculous closed loop of your voice again, repeating its happy hello.

"Please pick up," I said. "I know you're there."

THE OBSERVABLE UNIVERSE

THEY HAD BEEN TRANSFORMED by time and violence and peroxide.
Although Peter was heavier than when they had last seen each
other and his hair longer and tousled, the most noticeable changes
were the gouges along his forehead and the masklike circles around
his eyes. Gwen's hair was blonde instead of brown, a joyous color
that did not exist in nature, and cut short and intentionally messy, as
if she had been roughed up just a little bit too. "It looks like you've
been mugged," she said. "What happened to you?"

"I was mugged," he said.

Gwen wore army fatigues, combat boots, and a sweatshirt flecked
with every possible color of paint. She looked ready for prolonged
battle, real trench warfare stuff, and Peter imagined her stabbing her
paintbrush at the canvas as it if were every boyfriend that ever did
her wrong. "Come here," she said. "Let me hug you," and suddenly
he felt as small and fragile as when the first punch had knocked him
to one knee and the voice above him had said something about his
stupid-ass sneakers.

As a disembodied voice called out arrival and departure times,
his arms rose and encircled her. He closed his eyes and squeezed.

"What's that sound?" she asked.

He could feel her breath rising and falling against his chest. "I'm
crying," he said.

The bus spilled out passengers behind him—elderly women on fixed incomes meeting their children's children and teenagers with peach-fuzz beards. But they were not in such a hurry that they couldn't stop and stare. Let them look, he decided. He was almost proud of the bruises dotting his left arm. These were injuries people could understand.

It was a very *complicated* place they were going to, Gwen said. You had to drive away from it to get there. There were many spots like that in New Jersey, she explained, that you had to slide around, approach from odd angles. This was how the roads worked around here. You had to be crafty.

Gwen drove with one hand, drank a cup of coffee and smoked a cigarette with the other, and Peter felt perfectly, wonderfully safe.

"Shoot," she said. "That was the exit. I'll get the next one." She glanced over at him, drained her coffee and stuffed the cup between the emergency brake and the seat. "Are you sure you're okay?"

"I'm fine," he said. "Really."

"How much money did they get?"

"They didn't take any money." He thought of his sneakers, tied together at the laces, tossed over the telephone wires and left to dangle.

"Technically it's not a mugging then," Gwen said. "They were harassing you, which is worse. I wish I had been there."

When they were kids, Gwen would take on anybody for him, two or three boys at a time. He remembered her arms wind-milling, the bullies stumbling back, the occasional awkward headlock, the begging and pleading.

"Listen," she said. "I'm capturing it all for posterity on video tape.

138

If you're not up for it, you could stay at my place and we could watch it together tomorrow."

"No," Peter said. "I'm fine," and he closed his eyes and imagined his mother over-watering his plants, opening and reading his meager stack of mail, exploring his medicine cabinet. He thought of mentioning her to Gwen, but he knew where that would go. It was a short road from Mom to Dad.

"Are you sure?" she asked.

"Earl Schneider is going to be there, Gwen."

"I know. I know," she said, and then, "Who is Earl Schneider?"

He wouldn't privilege that with a response.

"Are you dressing up?" she finally asked, as she pushed the car up between two trucks.

"No," he said, and he touched his broken lip with his thumb.

The truth was, he felt like he was already wearing a costume. He fingered the deepest cut on his forehead and pictured the shock on his mother's face when he returned to Boston, and for the second time, he pushed her to the back of his mind. Let Gwen mention her first. She was her mother too.

He moved his feet around, trying to find a section of the rubber floor mat that wasn't sticky with a history of spilled soft drinks.

"Can we stop at a shoe store?" he said.

"Sure," she said. "Of course."

There was a pain deep in his stomach, as if he had swallowed a little pointed bone.

The Inter-Plex Accounting Solutions Sports and Convention Center loomed into view as they took the exit. It looked like something that might house the most important members of some futuristic government enclave, all smooth reflective surfaces and long white lines. Gwen had the appearance of someone who might be comfortable spending a good deal of time there. She wore thick dark sunglasses and she looked so beautiful and aloof that Peter wanted to hug her again and hold on tight. She pulled hard up to a stop sign, blasting through without turning her head. It seemed like a perfectly okay thing to do, statistically speaking.

It seemed not very long ago at all when Gwen had still been just his kid sister, poking her head into his room, reading his comic books over his shoulder, asking him tentative questions about the horror movies they watched on late night TV. She had been eight and he had been eleven when she had first dressed his Planet of the Apes action figures in Barbie's pink dresses. His father had thought that was hilarious. He had laughed so loud, Peter had caught a glimpse of his tongue. That had seemed as intimate as seeing him naked.

Sometimes Peter hated his father—not for doing what he did, but because he had passed on all the strands of genetic junk that made the same future seem like a possibility for his son. He looked over at Gwen, who was still driving one-handed, eyes invisible behind her shades. She must have felt him watching, because she turned and smiled at him. Somebody behind them beeped their horn, somebody in front of them too. She didn't seem to notice. "Mom called me earlier today," she said, with the superior attitude of someone who had just decided to forfeit a boring game. "She's worried about you. But what's new, right?"

There it was. Now they'd talk about Dad, just briefly, and then, as much to avoid that scary topic as anything else, she'd ask him about his moods, his living situation, his job at the gas station. Was he thinking about moving into his own place? After navigating that little minefield, there would be a pat on his thigh, a penetrating look into his face. "You were always the smarter of the two of us," she would say. How many times had he heard that?

He decided not to answer her.

"Are you sure you were mugged, Peter?" she asked. "Are you sure that's what happened to you? It seems a little strange. Why would they do that to you?"

"I wasn't mugged. You said so yourself."

"You know what I mean."

He wanted to tell her that sometimes his instincts about the world were right. As his knees had buckled, he had thought, *This is it, this is the end,* and he had almost welcomed it as the logical conclusion of the story his father had started years before.

The truly crazy thing was that his biology could make the sky seem so dark on certain days. His legs were so heavy in the morning, up there in the second floor apartment of his mother's house. The phone would ring nine, ten, eleven times. Finally he would give in, pick up the receiver, and listen to her voice ask him, "Are you okay?" He made a sound like he sometimes made at meals when she told him he should eat more, a grunt that signaled both *yes* and *no*. She always seemed so far away when he spoke to her on the phone, as if she were calling from the other side of the country and not the floor below him.

They drove in silence, staring at the convention center spiking the horizon. She was right. It definitely seemed to be moving further away. He reached out and adjusted the mirror on his side of the car so he could look at his face.

When he saw danger in the eyes of strangers on the street—felt it coiled inside jars and crouched behind doors and following him like it was his shadow—he tried not to be shocked by the unfairness of it, because it seemed like Gwen had received the other side, the side that brimmed with ideas and colors and one-hundred-mile-an-hour chatter, the side that had inspired his father to play with them on his hands and knees—to make silver go-go boots out of tinfoil and wrap them around the monkey action figure's feet, apply make-up with colored pencil, link him arm-in-arm with the Ken doll. It was at these times that his father was most likely to talk about how he had turned a corner. It was like speaking with the best salesman in the world, and Peter always opened the door to his heart and let him in again.

"Just so you know," Peter said quietly, as he watched the strip malls slide by to his right. "Earl Schneider is *the* creative mind behind *Space Wheel 2000*. That's who Earl Schneider is."

"*Space Wheel 2000?* Peter, this convention is going to last all weekend long. Forty-eight hours. Three floors. Forty thousand square feet. Sixty thousand square feet. Eighty thousand square feet."

"Okay," Peter said.

"My point is, this is not just about *Space Wheel 2000*. Compared to this, *Space Wheel 2000* is old news, Peter. Very old news. Stop living in the past. Compared to this, *Space Wheel 2000* is Columbus discovering America. It's Homo Halibus, Peter."

The cars streamed around them. It was beyond him how they didn't just careen into one another, sputter off the embankment, crash against the guardrails. He was making shuddering, rasping sounds at the back of his throat. "Pull over," he said. "I'm hyperventilating."

She did as she was told, and was polite enough not to look as he tried to calm himself down. When he was breathing normally, she waited, watching the cars slide by, and then she said, "We shouldn't be doing this. I'm turning around."

"No," he said. "I'm fine. Really."

She reached across his lap, opened the glove compartment. Beneath the maps and a pot baggie she found some wet naps, ripped them open with her teeth, and tried to push them across his face. "Let me at least clean you up."

He held up his hands to stop her. "Let's just go," he said. Reluctantly, she fell away from him, slapped the turn signal, and bolted out into traffic, moving the wet nap over her own face.

He had switched medications recently, then switched again, and then stopped altogether the day before yesterday. Maybe his mother had somehow deciphered that decision in his body language, in the way he held his head, chewed his food, answered her questions about the weather. Maybe that was why she had called Gwen.

He thought of his mother standing behind him in the basement, the clatter of the ball in the can of spray paint as he shook it, his silver sneakers spread on newspapers in front of him. "I was hoping you wouldn't be going under the circumstances," she had said. "Can't you call Gwen and explain to her that it's a bad time for you?"

It was always a bad time.

"Here we are," Gwen said, as she slowed for a speed bump.

It was unfair, too, that Gwen had been the one who could always reach their father when he was sitting at the kitchen table, staring at the hairs on the back of his hands, and unfair, in a way, that she could reach Peter in the same way, with a smile or a joke or her art. That's what her experiments with his action figures had been—the first burp of her artistic tendencies. All her other art seemed to follow from those days, zoom, in a straight line.

They parked the car and walked across the hot parking lot. Man, his head hurt all of a sudden. A 24oz. Pepsi seemed like a good idea, maybe a basket of fries criss-crossed with catsup.

He stopped and steeled himself to cross the street. He hated crossing streets. When she held up her hand, palm-open like a traffic cop, the cars stopped short. She took the first step, pulling him along. "Come on," she said. She gave his hand a squeeze and they followed the sidewalk around the corner toward the entrance. "This still makes me feel like a little kid," she said. "Does it still make you feel like a little kid, Peter?"

In some ways, he *always* felt like a little kid. At twenty-eight years old, Peter couldn't see these pilgrimages stopping anytime soon, even when Gwen dropped out, which she would soon. The video camera was a step back, a way to be an objective observer. She was on her way out. "Look at that," she said. She smiled and pointed out someone with an opaque space bubble on her head, golden skin, skin-tight cat suit, four-inch heels. They jumped up on the curb and fell in line behind her, following her sexy walk past the signs advertising bad rock concerts and the Harlem Globetrotters for one night only.

"Yeah," he said, and his anger pivoted from his father—hiding back there in the tunnel of the past—to his sister, who was standing right next him, holding his hand. Did she think that this was all he needed? A party atmosphere, some daily application of will power, a little get up and go? But he had to admire the costume. It must have taken weeks of work. He zippered his jacket up his stomach and quickened his pace to match her own.

They joined up with a few others walking in the same direction, some dressed fantastically, some not. Everybody was either smiling or putting on their serious sci-fi attitudes, chins lifted ten degrees too high, strides a little too long. Most of them didn't often get this chance, so it was easy to forgive them. They were all beautiful, here, in their natural habitats.

It took him a minute to realize a few people were staring—two girls dressed as green Siamese twins, a kid in a long black coat holding a plastic sword, some sentimental throwback with Vulcan ears.

"Man," the first Siamese twin said to him. "You did a great job on your make-up."

"What are you supposed to be?" the other head asked.

Matthew said, "It's one of the open secrets of science fiction conventions. Costumes are *not* disguises. They are emblems of a person's true self. It's the three-piece suit, the ugly tie, the sensible skirt, these are the things that mask who we truly are. But these heroic figures around us, they are the displays of the person's inner life."

Yes, that's what Peter should have told the twins.

Matthew was dressed in a long metallic cape and goggles, his double-knotted combat boots spray-painted silver. His hair was slicked back on his head, just like Peter had been planning to do to his own, back when the idea of going to the convention dressed as a character from *Space Wheel 2000* still seemed like a possibility.

They had found Matthew in the crowd and—pulled along in the wake of Gwen's personality—made some quick introductions. "You're dressed as one of my brother's favorite characters," Gwen had said.

When they were kids the Zen-Force Soldiers had been the coolest of all the cool characters populating the show. Their lack of emotion allowed them to remain serene when everything around them was chaos. Often Peter had put both palms together and closed his eyes, sitting on his bedroom floor, trying to make the world drop away in the same manner the soldiers did just before they entered battle.

145

Seeing this man, Matthew, dressed as one—dressed as Peter had planned to dress—should have made him happy, but it didn't.

"We should keep the line moving," he said.

"Cuts?" Gwen asked, and Matthew made space for them as if they were old friends.

As they stood in line, Peter looked Matthew over more closely. Some aspects of his costume were even better than his own. The boots, for instance. Much better than the sneakers. But Matthew didn't need to know that. "I can see everything with these on," he said, as he raised his head and scanned the sky and then down along the long line of people waiting to be admitted.

"I can see everything too," Peter said, as he looked around. Who was minding the children who were running up and down the sidewalk, waving plastic light sabers?

"What do you think so far?" Matthew asked.

"It's very interesting," Peter said.

"It's so like what you expected that it's nothing like what you expected. That's what you're saying. You're saying it feeds into your preconceptions so much that it challenges them."

"I've been to a couple dozen of these things," Peter said. "I'm not a newbie."

"This is my eighty-first," Matthew said and he lifted up his goggles onto his forehead, inspecting Peter with his own eyes now. Why did he have the urge to ask this guy about his upbringing?

Gwen raised the video camera to her eye and panned along the crowd, pausing on especially good costumes or especially bad costumes, and then moving on to the next person. "I think it's more complicated than that, Matthew," she explained. "I think you were right and you were wrong when you said the costumes weren't

146

disguises. Clichés can be comforting to the person living them, whether it's the cliché of the fifty-year-old man in the business suit or the guy dressed as a Wookie. It's all part of the same thing." She reached up and zoomed in on a guy with an exposed brain as she said this, as if she were narrating her film as she filmed it.

Peter thought of himself, age eight, a blanket wrapped around his shoulders, his father at the kitchen table, playing his infinite games of solitaire. "What?" he asked, mostly because he just wanted to hear her voice rambling, the way she did in bed when they were kids, speaking out into the dark, making it up as she went along.

"Clichés," she said, "can be comforting disguises. The all-powerful businessman. The earth mother. The virgin. The whore." She gestured extravagantly to a fat guy in a Batman costume. "The superhero." She turned back to Peter. "The victim."

They were almost to the entrance. Up ahead, he could see two security officers. They were frisking people, spreading their arms like wings, sliding their hands down their tinfoil bodies.

He thought of Gwen at the kitchen table during those solitaire games, watching her father's hands.

"Look at that," Matthew said. "Jesus. Do they think we're idiots?"

A large green poster at the entrance announced two of the seven screenwriters who worked on the American *Godzilla* were making an appearance today, discussing their craft and signing copies of the DVD. "How horrible," Gwen said. "I saw it twice, for some reason, and it was even worse the second time." She scanned the camera over the poster, and then slowly over Matthew's face, absorbing his disgusted reaction.

"I've always been a *King Kong* man myself," Peter said. "It's more pure. None of this remake stupidity."

"They did remake *King Kong*," Matthew said, "and it was awful. Remember? It starred Jessica Lang. It was totally ridiculous. And there are rumors of an even newer version. From the guy who did *Lord of the Rings*. He's looking for a new franchise, I guess."

"Peter Jackson," Peter said.

"Whatever," Matthew said. "It's going to be *such* a bomb."

"Yeah, well," Peter said. "King Kong is still the better character. You have to admit that."

It was taking real effort to speak, to move his mouth and form the words. He wished he hadn't been so foolhardy and flushed the meds. But it had seemed like a great thing at the time, a blow against all the cures that had failed him and a blow against his mother's protectiveness. Maybe a blow against himself too. The pills had swirled around the toilet and then vanished and he had imagined them sliding down the pipes in the house, down the wall behind his mother's head as she sat flipping through her *Reader's Digest*.

"I don't have to admit anything," Matthew said. "What you have on the one hand is a six hundred foot tall bullet-proof dinosaur who breathes radioactive fire. Then you have, in this corner, a forty-foot monkey. Where's the debate? There is no debate at all."

"That's not what I'm talking about," Peter said, his voice rising. "I'm not talking about who would win in a fight. That's kiddy stuff."

It was his turn to spread his arms. He winced when the security officer touched his stomach, partly from the pain, partly from the idea of being touched by a stranger.

He imagined the room beyond the entrance as a small chamber, the size and smell of a service elevator, the people pushing together, jockeying for valuable floor space. He told himself this was not true, of course, but the thought wouldn't go away. It had taken occupancy in his head and there was no way to ignore it, and no way to verbalize it either. Gwen was smiling, turning in a circle as the security officer looked her over. "You're what's her name," the officer said. "That multimedia artist."

"That's right," she said. "I'm what's her name." Was she flirting with him? It was hard to tell. His head was shaved bald and Peter could see little flaps on the back of his neck where the skin bunched up. He looked like he lifted barbells in his bedroom, ate with his face close to the plate, had untroubled dreams about beautiful girls. Peter hated people like that.

"Well, then, who do you think would win then?" Matthew asked him, and Peter looked away from Gwen, across Matthew's silver body, forcing himself to take him all in. The thumb and two fingers of his right hand were wrapped in band-aids, as if he were ready to play the banjo. He had been biting his fingernails, Peter guessed. A nervous person.

"Well, nobody wins in a situation like that," Peter said.

Matthew tapped his bandaged thumb and finger together as if to some secret music playing only for him, talking over the head of the security officer who was kneeling and checking out his boots. "What do you mean nobody wins in a situation like that? I'm talking about Godzilla and King Kong," he said. "What are you talking about?"

"Nobody wins in that kind of fight. Not the two principal monsters and not the people living around the site of the battle. That's a subtext to all those giant monster movies."

"Wait a second, Ghandi," Matthew said. "Let me give you an example of what I mean. This should help clear things up. The Empire State Building. He climbed the whole thing, right? Pretty amazing." His fingers spider-walked up the air. "Well, Godzilla is as big as the whole building." He smiled and laughed and folded his arms across his narrow chest.

"Fine," Peter said. "Great."

"Don't agree with me just to end the conversation," Matthew said. "Agree with me because I'm right."

"Okay," Peter said. "You're right."

"You're just saying that," Matthew said.

Lines of tables filled the main hall. For a couple hundred bucks a pop, people could rent these tables for the day to sell whatever they wanted to sell and sign whatever they needed to sign. Small clusters of artists sold comic book drawings and caricatures, grizzled men bartered over trading cards, and other people seemed to be trying to unload whatever they had found in the closet that morning.

They did a quick reconnaissance around the tables. At a larger booth, two men were demonstrating expensive little gadgets: watches that took your pulse, battery-operated hats that warmed your head, cell phones seemingly the size of paperclips. "Hey, hey, hey," one of them said to him, "you look like a smart guy," but Peter floated past without answering.

The other salesperson was videotaping people with a hand-held video camera, zooming in on them, panning back. Their images appeared on a TV behind him. Peter saw himself there, just for a moment, in living color, lip swollen, one nostril encrusted with dried blood. He wondered if people thought he was dressed as a zombie. "You're famous," the salesman with the camera said, which is what he was saying to everybody who appeared on the TV. "You're a star."

Gwen stepped out from behind Matthew and up to the salesman, gazing at him through the lens of her video camera. At first, he seemed taken aback by this reversal of power, but then he lifted his camera again and tilted it toward her. They stood there for a while, meditatively filming each other, sliding the camera over each other's bodies.

"Over here," Matthew said.

"No," Peter said, as he noticed the time. "I have to find one of the conference rooms."

"This will just take a second."

Some of the artists would sketch pictures of whatever you wanted for a small fee. "Draw me and my friend here," Matthew said to the closest one, who was finishing up a drawing of a shirtless soldier holding a very big gun. It took the artist no more than three minutes to slash some lines across the piece of paper, and then he held it up noncommittally, as if he had found it instead of created it.

It wasn't very good. In the drawing, Peter's blackened eyes did not look like blackened eyes. He simply looked incredibly tired, as if he had gone without sleep for two, three, four days. He looked thinner, too, and he was smiling in a way he had never smiled—so happily as to be almost manic. Jesus, he looked like his father.

"Great," Matthew said, "now draw just me, but stronger. Like The Hulk. Show me lifting a truck. With one hand. And make me look angry."

The artist lowered his head and began to draw.

There were spaceships suspended by wire, men dressed as robots, replicas of every character featured on every science fiction show ever made. The further they moved into the future, the deeper they moved into Peter's past. He was aware of the irony—if that was the right word for it.

There was no sign on the door, but they found the room by trial and error and sat near the back, where they listened to the speaker. He was a thin elderly man who sneered occasionally as he talked and banged his hand softly on the podium at the end of sentences, and at first, Peter didn't recognize him. Still, despite his age, he looked proud, as if he had survived a terrible event long ago. Matthew flipped his goggles up on his forehead and leaned forward to hear. "Which is when they brought in the new writers," the old man was saying, as his sneer slid open into a smile of contempt.

"Who is that?" Peter whispered to Matthew.

"That's Earl Schneider."

"Who?"

"Earl Schneider. He was one of the two major creative minds behind *Space Wheel 2000*, the other being the very talented and very dead Martin Page."

Peter had only ever seen Earl Schneider in old publicity photos. He looked at the old man again, as if seeing him for the first time. He had heard the word survivor used to describe everybody from aging soul divas to movie actors with strings of bombs to their credit, but this person was the first who looked like he deserved the title. His glasses, Peter noticed, were slightly crooked on his face.

The auditorium was flecked with people. Some of them were reading. A few were whispering into cell phones. One stood up, wiped his hands on his jeans, and exited, the door slamming behind him. After a moment the clang of another metal door could be heard from down the hall.

Matthew moved in closer. Peter could smell something thick and mustardy on his breath. "It's Schneider's contention that *Space Wheel 2000* was never really *Space Wheel 2000* after the third episode, which is when the powers-that-be neutered his creative control."

"Simple betrayal," the man at the podium said, and he threw up his arms, stepped back, as if he was finished, and then stepped forward. Looking out over the crowd, he said in a softer voice, "I urge you not to support episodes four through nine. You might as well support *The Love Boat* or *Three's Company* if you do. You might as well support fascism."

Peter noticed an obese man in the front wearing an undersized T-shirt. The man stared up at the podium with a look of squint-eyed determination, and when Earl Schneider asked, "Are there any questions?" his hand was already stretched into the air, as if straining for something out of his reach.

"This schism you're talking about," the man in the audience said. "I think it really developed after episode two. I think that's really where the rift is."

"Episode three is still valid," Earl Schneider said in a weary way, as if he has heard this before, heard it a million times. "And furthermore, that is not a question." His gaze searched the room. "Are there any actual questions? Anything at all?"

"I have a question," Peter found himself saying. A few people turned around to look.

"Yes?"

Peter couldn't speak. The silence was frightening, but there was nothing he could do. The words hadn't reached his lips yet. They were forming somewhere inside him, down where the pain was sliding around. He could feel it. Matthew fingered his goggles, and Earl Schneider asked again, more quickly, "What is your question?"

"How do you do it?" he asked, and he swallowed hard. He rubbed sweat out of his eyes.

"Excuse me?"

Peter imagined Earl Schneider carrying his small television show like an albatross down through the years, bearing its weight for so long that its failure became a strange kind of success.

All eyes were on him now. He wondered if he was going to vomit, and if so, what he would vomit. "I have always loved your show," he said, attempting to backtrack. "It was a solace to me in my childhood. It's a solace to me now."

He thought of how the ancient somebodies used to make sense of the world by looking at sheep and chicken guts. What secrets would his own messy insides contain if he emptied his stomach out onto the polished floor of the Inter-Plex Accounting Solutions Sport and Convention Center?

If he was thinking thoughts like that, he knew he was in a little trouble. Those were the kind of thoughts he had on the worst mornings. Strange how they could be funny and terrifying at the same time, how humor became horror if you let it spin around in your head too much. He thought of his father pacing the kitchen, laughing at jokes nobody else could hear.

"When I was a kid," he started, and then he stopped, remembering his father's face—his dad's face, he corrected himself, because he had never called him father when he was alive. He remembered the way his dad's face slid from pain to a sly little smile and how he had wondered what had been going on behind there that might make him that way. "How do you keep going?" he asked.

He swallowed again, rested his hand on the back of the folding chair in front of him and pushed himself to a standing position. Matthew looked up at him. Everyone looked up at him except for Earl Schneider, who looked down at him from the podium as if he were a fly, a turd, a distraction that would be dealt with momentarily. He narrowed his eyes and said, "What exactly are you getting at?"

Just that he was in pain. It was getting very hard for him to breath and something strange and dangerous was happening inside him. "I'm not sure," he said. "I just love your show. It was more of a solace than you could ever know. I watched a lot of television growing up. I still do. But your show stands out."

Earl Schneider moved out to the lip of the stage, fingering the clip-mike attached to his tie. Peter noticed that he was not well-dressed, that his shirt was bunched at his waist and his pants were worn, sacrifices he had made for the cause. Peter pictured him wandering the country, preaching his message, full of bitterness and devotion and purpose, and for a second Earl Schneider was everything Peter was not, a traveler from a strange and different place.

"Any other questions?" Earl Schneider asked.

No, he didn't have anymore questions.

But he had something else to say.

His father had not been capable of the foresight or kindness to do it gently. He had not thought about who would find him afterward, although he had written a long, lucid note detailing their finances, which were well taken care of due to what he called his "early successes in the world." The handwriting had been simple block letters from his training as an engineer; Peter had thought it was a joke until he had gone into the bathroom, because it had been too neat to be a suicide note.

It suddenly seemed very important that Earl Schneider should know all of this, or at least that someone should, that Peter should talk about it with someone who had lived it with him. He opened his mouth to speak it.

"The fat guy was right about episode three," Matthew muttered. "It's a complete piece of shit."

Peter turned to find Matthew—to tell him to be quiet—but the act of turning had become something else in mid-motion; it had become *staggering,* it had become *lurching,* and Peter couldn't find the source of Matthew's voice anyway, because it was suddenly coming from far, far away, as if Peter were standing on a building's ledge and Matthew were shouting up from the street below. And he closed his eyes and then they were touching him—fingers poked his chest and stroked his head—and Matthew's distant grumble became his sister's voice, whispering to him, telling him everything was going to be okay and he should just be still.

All dramatic moments happen as if captured on film. They speed up. They slow down. They're shot in a frenzy of multiple angles. They happen for posterity, offer themselves up for deliberation. He was falling, and what was the word for the look on his face?

There was something beautiful about the way he kicked out the chair and tumbled to the carpet. His cheek touched the rug and people looked away from Earl Schneider and toward him. He had become the convention's most popular attraction.

And this was the best part.

In the moment after Peter fell, the camera view tilted up to the crisscrossed metal framework of the ceiling as Gwen handed it to someone next to her. And then Matthew stepped into frame, just for a moment, took the camera, and steadied it, focused it, pivoted it back in Peter's direction. He was capturing every nuance of the event—the opening of Peter's mouth, the closing of his eyes, Gwen crouching next to him and running her hands along his scalp. He was speaking over the scene, talking to someone next to him. "Where's the zoom?" he asked, as Gwen touched Peter's face, swept back his hair from his forehead.

She must not have known what else to do—what other comfort to give him—except to neaten his hair, as if his picture were about to be taken. Which it was. The camera zeroed in for a close-up. Peter's eyes opened and looked into the lens, into his other set of eyes, which were looking back at him from Gwen's couch, not far into the future.

A bystander had a responsibility to a moment like that. A bystander has to ask, what am I seeing? Peter was that bystander, as he watched himself fall for the second time on Gwen's living room television.

A woman in a flowing silver robe and bald wig said, "I'm a nurse," and the image went black.

"Again?" Gwen said. She was the one holding the remote control. Her other hand, her left, touched Peter's arm. He took the control from her and hit a button. He was sitting on the couch, pillow jammed down in the small of his back, plastic cup of juice in his hand.

The cut on his forehead had been given two neat stitches, although the doctor at outpatient had explained that there wasn't much they could do for his bruised ribs. "Try not to expose yourself to jokes," he had said. "It's going to hurt when you laugh," and then he had chuckled himself, as if the warning itself had been a joke.

When he had finished with the doctor, Peter had emerged into the reception area to find Gwen standing by the long, dark hospital window, watching the headlights sliding around in the parking lot. They had walked to the car without speaking. "Matthew wanted to come too," she had explained, as she turned the key in the ignition, "but I told him to stay at the convention."

They had driven to her apartment, talking about the patience and kindness of the hospital staff, and when they had arrived there, they had plugged her camera into her VCR with a long cable that rested coiled on the TV. The first thing he had noticed as he sat down were the paintings hanging everywhere—swirls of colors and strange perspectives, squares inside squares, beautiful splashes of light.

Gwen had popped in the tape and they had watched it and then watched it again. They were still watching it.

He had been a tourist in his father's pain for a long time; he lacked the imagination and fortitude to really live there. But new vistas were opening inside him. He could envision some interesting things happening with his life. His death, for instance. It was right there on the TV.

His open mouth and closed eyes. His bloody forehead. The pinched worry in the face of his sister, and the baby-blank acceptance in his own. The gasping for breath and the flutter of the eyes as they twitched open and saw nothing he could really remember. Was this more intimate? Was this knowledge? He wasn't sure. They watched the images again in silence, and when the screen turned to black and then to static, Gwen reached out and touched his hand. Her fingers slid across his palm and then the buttons of the remote control. The tape clicked to a stop. "I think that's enough?" she asked.

"Once more," he said. His finger found the start button and the tape spooled forward into its first images—the entrance to the convention center, the long lines of people, and then his own face, slowly pulled closer by the zoom, giving the eye of the lens a wary look. "Here I am again," Peter said. "Right here."

TORTURE ME

HE COULD HEAR THE SLAM OF THE CAR DOOR, the opening and closing of the trunk. They were back from shopping and he had his underwear around his ankles, his hand on the remote control. But he wasn't frightened or even shocked. Some part of him—the tiny gossamer self that seemed to float above his head at moments like this—even found it kind of funny.

He set the remote on the arm of the sofa, stood up, and tugged up his pants. The images were still flickering on the TV, demanding his attention. While Elizabeth and Danny were opening the door, he would be popping the tape out of the VCR, heading up the stairs. While they were entering the kitchen he would be coming down, smiling, a sweater pulled on over his head, his hand making a swipe through his hair.

On the TV screen, three men stood in a triangle. In a moment the camera would zoom in on the largest one, his ski-masked face, his bland eyes looking downward at the source of the voice that was just now beginning to speak the words she always spoke at this moment.

Three syllables. Part command, part plea, part incantation. He didn't know if it had been scripted or improvised or even if it was her voice or something dubbed in later. Her mouth was open as if to receive a kiss. The shaking camera toggled down and inward.

He flipped his wrist as he walked across the room, saw that it wasn't quite four. They weren't supposed to be back until five. Sheridan could hear Danny's feet clip-clopping on the porch. His son had recently reached the age of daring, and was constantly trying to commit small acts of courage, which at the moment meant trying to take steps two at a time. Sheridan could hear Elizabeth yelling after him. She was probably trying to get packages out of the car—groceries, some new clothes, and some present meant to appease Danny as she dragged him from store to store. "Chill out," she yelled.

He hit stop, jerked the video from the recorder. He had only just started and he visualized the images he had yet to see—the most vivid ones, the ones he watched the tape for—spooled up on the right side. He hated not rewinding a video. It was a sin against order, like leaving your shoes in the hallway or dirty dishes in the sink.

He was walking to the stairs.

As a sort of joke he took them two at a time.

But also: He had to, because they were spilling into the kitchen, Danny running into the dining room waving something. Sheridan caught the object out of the corner of his eye, but did not wait to identify it.

"Dad," Danny's voice called out. "We're home."

"I'm upstairs on the computer," Sheridan called back.

He didn't have time to put the videotape in its usual place so he threw it under some papers on his desk. Then he dropped back into his chair, hands on the keyboard. Which is where Danny found him. He ran around the corner, head bowed, and plowed into him, so that his forehead struck against his raised elbow. But Danny didn't seem to register any pain. "I got a banana," he said, and he held it out to him like a sword. That's what he had been waving around—Elizabeth must have bought it for him.

It could make a person's heart swell, the simple tricks Elizabeth performed to make their son happy. Sheridan said, "Did you have fun?"

"Kind of," Danny said, thoughtfully, as if this were a question he really, really had to consider carefully. "We stopped and got gasoline." Sheridan pictured them standing at the gas station, Elizabeth explaining how the pumps worked, the way the gasoline snaked up from the ground and through the hose, Danny solemnly watching the numbers spin higher as the tank filled.

"Want to help me in the kitchen?" Sheridan asked.

He made a more elaborate meal than he had planned: vegetarian lasagna with a light cream sauce, a side of carrots sprinkled with cinnamon, some bread split with butter. He even opened a bottle of red wine and made a show of pouring it, lifting it in the air to eye-level and letting a stream splash down into the glass. "What are we celebrating?" Elizabeth asked.

"Sunday night, I guess," he said.

They sat down to eat. He saw a flash of hand-motion and heard a soft thump from the corner of the room.

"Danny," he said. "What did I tell you about the dog?"

His son liked to throw food in the dog's general direction. He would cup a ball of squished bread in his hand, look to his left, and throw to his right, striking the wall, the floor, sometimes the edge of the dog's water dish. It was an obvious act, but also clandestine—not once had he admitted to ever doing it. Sometimes he threw carrots or cubes of steak, potato skins or applesauce, and then shook his head *no, no, no,* each word rising in volume.

"Don't do it again, okay?" Sheridan said.

"What?" Danny said, and wiped his palms together.

In bed that night Sheridan spooned with Elizabeth, one arm around her, rubbing her tummy through her undershirt. "I ate too much," she said. "I was eating and I thought to myself, I'm eating too much, but I didn't stop. I thought, I'm still eating too much, and I just kept going."

He pressed two fingers against her abdomen—gentle steady pressure. Then he moved to her back, working down the spine and then up between the shoulder blades. He always found complex knots there, tensions that could be traced to specific arguments and worries. The human body, he thought, was a map of such experiences. Long after something had dropped from the mind it still might reside in vertebrae and muscle.

It was not something he talked about very often because if he let himself go on about it the idea began to sound ridiculous.

After a few minutes of attention he could feel her relaxing. He kissed her on the ear and told her that he loved her, and then told her again because he realized she was asleep. He liked to say sentimental things to her when she was sleeping. It was a tradition that went back a decade, to when they were first dating and they'd go on camping trips. The first time he told her he loved her was when she was sleeping; the second and third times as well. It had been a kind of rehearsal.

She made a guttural noise and gathered herself inward, chest toward stomach.

"Sorry," he said, and then he curled in his own direction.

It snowed most of the night—a driving, wet snow that hardened across the windshield and up under the wheel wells of the truck—and Sheridan was ten minutes late to work the next morning. He entered

162

through the front door and walked to the back of the clinic, to find the lights on and Mrs. Hayford reclined on one of the weight benches, pulling small barbells up and across her chest. "You shouldn't have started without me," he said, with as much congeniality as he could gather considering that just a half hour before he had been slamming a shovel down into a frozen wall pushed across the front of his driveway by a passing snowplow.

Sheila shouldn't have *let* her start without him. She shouldn't have even let her back here. But Sheila wasn't even at the front desk. The place seemed deserted except for Mrs. Hayford. How had she even made it here?

"I have the routine memorized," she said, as the two weights clicked together at the height of their arc. She began to lower them again, her arms shaking slightly.

"Actually," he said, as he walked over to her, "you're overextending your arms. And you should be using three-pounders—the lime green ones, remember? You told me it was your favorite color." He touched her arm and helped guide the weight to its proper position directly above her chest.

"They all look the same to me," she said.

"I can see that," he said. He noticed that she must have lifted and tried out five or six weights before settling on the ones she held. Some had been placed in the wrong slots, others on the floor, and he had to close and open his eyes to still his annoyance. He hadn't taken off his wet coat, so he tugged it from his shoulders and placed it on the weight bench next to hers. There would be a lot of cancellations and he'd have more time to work with her on her form.

Some of the elderly clients had difficulty completing more than four or five repetitions of the same exercise. It was not so much their physical frailty as their lack of concentration, what another one of the physical therapists called the inability to see anything through a ten count. A lot of them wanted to tell stories—observations about how things had changed in this part of town in the last twenty-five years. Most of the women related anecdotes about their children and some of the men had war stories, and all of them related them in a roundabout way, as if daring the listener to sort it all out. Sheridan considered it part of his job to listen, to laugh if the stories were funny or to nod and say, "I know. It's a shame," if they were serious. But he was interested too, more interested than he sometimes felt he should be.

Which brought him back to the idea of concentration. The central effort of his job, he had decided long ago, involved sustaining the focus needed to see someone as a human being.

"That's good," he told her. "Up you go."

Last week Mrs. Hayford told him about a trip she had taken to Cape Breton as a child. Her father had been some kind of corporate executive and they had traveled extensively when she was a girl. She had visited France as a ten-year-old, she said, been to Germany and Spain too, but Cape Breton had been her favorite. They had driven—on most of their trips they had flown—and because of the long drive from Connecticut through Canada, she had thought it was the furthest away, the most exotic.

The water off the coast of Cape Breton Isle was surprisingly warm and she and her sister waded out for what seemed like a half mile before they had to paddle instead of walk. From the shore they looked back at their parents, no more than little shadows on the beach. The cliff walls hung behind them like a great black tapestry.

"I wasn't worried about myself," she said as Sheridan slid the heating pad in place between her shoulder blades. "I was worried for them. It seemed like we were going someplace special and we were leaving them behind."

Now she lived in a housing project on Summer Street. Sheridan knew the area. Across the street kids played basketball at a hoop with a red, white and blue net, and if you stopped your car there they would slide up next to it and ask you if you needed anything. The project itself was modest but nice, with flowerboxes in some of the windows. In the winter it looked worse than in the summer, when the flowers were blooming and there was more activity up and down the street. A square brick building never looked good in the snow.

"It's not what I had planned," she told him once.

She was in her late sixties, suffered from severe degenerative disc disorder in her upper vertebrae which caused her magnificent amounts of pain. She had used that word—*magnificent*—when first describing it to Sheridan, and he had asked her to give it a number from one to ten, ten being the worst.

She had looked at him like he had asked her to rate a symphony with a letter grade.

"Down," he said now. "Slower."

She had been a smoker all her adult life—until last month. Sheridan had convinced her to quit, first by teasing her, then by daring her. She was smart enough to know she was being manipulated but also smart enough to know that giving into the manipulation was in her best interest.

Two of the other therapists specialized in sports injuries, and it was inspiring to see their clients lose their limps, mend their knees, and erase the history of whatever accident had occurred on the court or ball field. But most of Sheridan's clients had begun a slow decline brought about by age, obesity, and bad choices, and the rewards were subtler, the dramatic progressions displaced by little bunny hops forward. Mostly he tried to mitigate pain, offer encouragement, and not expect too much.

"Great," he said. "Just stop at the very top of the arc."

"It's easier this way," she said as she corrected the motion. "Not painful."

"Nothing we do here should be painful," he said. "If it's painful then we're doing it wrong."

He used the word *we* whenever he could.

"You need to eat better," he said. "You're still losing weight."

"I don't like food anymore," she said.

"None of that," he said. He had heard it before. She guessed that she survived on coffee and cookies. "I'll give you some recipes," he added, a little more softly.

"I would appreciate it," she said.

"Excuse me," he said, because he noticed water was collecting around his boots. He kept spare sneakers and track pants in the back room.

He placed his boots upside down near the baseboard heating, unbuttoned his pants, and kicked them off. He put on his track pants while standing up, his head turned slightly in order to see himself in the mirror, because he suddenly felt tired and he wanted to know if he looked it. Which he did. He did not look completely like himself.

He was kneeling, tying the laces of his sneakers, when he heard Mrs. Hayford say, "Now my right shoulder hurts."

She had completed her repetitions and then followed him back here.

Usually it was the left that hurt. At least that's what she claimed. Possibly the pain was more mysteriously distributed. It often was. He thought of giving her new forms to complete, the small numbers to circle in blue pen, the little diagrams of the human body, simple as children's art. He gave the laces a final tug, stood, and stewarded her back out to the gym area. Sheila was there, looking apologetic. "I'm sorry," she said. "I was in the bathroom."

"We should probably just close for the morning," he said, as they walked back out to the reception area, leaving Mrs. Hayford to her exercise. "I have to catch up on some paperwork anyway."

"They'll come, you know," Sheila said.

"Oh, they love their therapy," he said, and he laughed.

"Lonely," she said, which was true.

So he stayed and when it was Mrs. Hayford's time to leave, he asked her if she could call Sheila when she got home, just to let them know she had arrived safely. He stood by the window watching her push snow from the rear windshield of her car. The wind was still blowing hard and occasionally she put her hand to the top of her head to hold her hat on. When she did this she stared out across the expanse of parking lot, as if she had spotted someone else in a similar predicament, but she was the only moving shape as far as Sheridan could tell. He hoped she might turn and notice him watching.

"Is it getting worse out there?" Sheila asked.

Sheridan kept himself in good shape. He swam every day at the high school pool during what they called citizen's hours, which were two small windows of opportunity, one at the very beginning of the day before the students arrived, another at the end when they had all gone home. If Sheridan missed the first then guilt almost always drove him to catch the second, and it wasn't that often that he missed the first anyway.

Each swim cost exactly one dollar, which he paid to the lifeguard—a high school student—who then placed it in a small metal box. At most there were usually three or four swimmers there, usually elderly men, but often Sheridan was the only one, and he enjoyed these laps the most for some reason he couldn't quite understand. He thought it might be a failing on his part to enjoy aloneness that much, especially when that aloneness was not much different than swimming laps with others.

Although maybe it was different, because his aloneness had a sharpness to it, a little like the swimming itself, the shape his body made cutting through the water. When he left the pool in the morning, hair still wet, the lights in the school parking lot were often still on and he had the sense of stealing an hour from God or fate. Or at least using an hour that had been given to him for sleep and finding a better use for it. He sometimes jogged to his truck, keys in his hand. It was almost the same in the evening, when the only other people around were a few students who stayed late for their sports.

So when he stopped on his way home work and noticed that the pool was closed, he felt as if something had been stolen from him— or more precisely, stolen back from him—and he made sure the doors were locked by gripping the double handle and tugging twice. They were chained and padlocked from the inside. He could tell from the give of the doors, the rattle of metal.

School must have been canceled today. He trudged back to his truck, which was still running by the curb, and decided since he had not kept one of his good habits, maybe he would do something with his bad one. The shop would be open—it never closed, not even on Christmas—and it was a twenty-five minute drive there, a twenty-five minute drive back. Less time than it usually took him to swim, shower, and get home. On the way back he could even stop at the grocery store and pick up some fresh Romaine lettuce for a salad. Elizabeth had said she was in the mood for greens.

Instead he went to the grocery store first. It was not a decision or even an impulse as much as a floating kind of randomness. He ended up in the turn-only lane and moved up to the red light, signaled, turned, and there he was, heading toward the store. He thought of spinning around the lot and heading out again but there was a good spot one slot over from a handicapped space and that good luck was enough to beckon him forward.

At the store he piled tomatoes, lettuce, carrots, more sweet potatoes than he needed, and boxes of raisins into a basket and when he found he didn't have enough room, he headed to the front of the store for a cart. That's where he noticed the vitamins in the health food section, and he sorted through them slowly, turning them around, imagining the glossy golden egg shape of the vitamin E as he put two bottles in his cart. Then others too. They were having a sale.

It was an odd form of gluttony, buying this many vitamins. He had never done anything like it before. It made him feel like a different person, someone who might be capable of doing other unexpected things too.

"Health nut," the woman said.

She must have been in her mid-twenties, her blonde hair cut close to her head. Her hands were folded in a gesture of politeness that instantly struck him as old-fashioned. She was pale and thin and seemed familiar. Sheridan either knew her in a casual way or knew her type.

169

"Leave some for me," she said.

He smiled and said, "Sorry. It's a good sale. I've never seen them this cheap."

She reached past him for some B–12. "I might stock up too," she said.

He was in his truck, turning the key in the ignition, when he realized why she had seemed familiar. It was that submissive gesture: hands folded in front, each finger touching each corresponding finger on the other hand. He had seen it over and over—delicate enough that it seemed contrived, the pose of an actor waiting for her next instructions. The woman in the grocery store had been acting too—flirting—because she knew there would be no consequence to their short conversation. So the thing that made their connection possible was also the thing that made it so unsatisfying—the falseness of it. And as he drove, she became as much an intrusion in the privacy of his thoughts as a stranger in the next lane of the pool. He wondered if Elizabeth had similar interactions as she moved through her day, and although he expected to feel a twinge of jealousy at the idea, he felt nothing except a longing to be with her, as if they had been separated much longer than just one day.

The route Elizabeth usually took when shopping cut through a small stretch of woods on the way from one set of strip malls in Massachusetts to another larger set in New Hampshire. They had once spotted a deer standing in the middle of that road, its neck craned as if listening to distant music, and they had slowed the car and then stopped, a line of vehicles forming behind them. Nobody had honked their horns or even nudged forward, and when the deer moved into the brush the line slid into motion slowly like a funeral procession. Today, though, Sheridan was alone, and he didn't even know why he had chosen this route, because it was taking him away from home in almost a straight line. Up ahead he spotted the gas station where Elizabeth and Danny had probably stopped the day before. Although she loved to shovel snow and chop wood, she hated pumping gas, but Danny would have begged her to turn in even though the tank was half-full.

At the intersection a single car blinked its high beams, signaling for him to go on ahead. He blinked his headlights too—simultaneously—and they both nudged forward comically before stopping, the nose of each vehicle poking into the intersection. He waved his hand and the other car took a left. He took a right and followed. The car was heading toward the stretch of apartments and old age homes near the river.

What had Elizabeth said? It had stuck with him for a while but now he couldn't remember it. Something about the way the deer stood and the patience of the people as they sat in their cars. That was before Danny was born, although she had been pregnant, and he remembered thinking that her comment had something to do with her pregnancy—that it showed insight acquired from this new stage in her life. They had been going out to a fancy dinner and he had been wearing a suit jacket. She had been wearing a dress, her tummy a small slope he sometimes touched with his palm.

He slowed to a stop and reversed slowly into a parking space and sat there for a long time letting the engine idle, listening to the man on the radio talk about some kind of contest. Then he climbed from the car and walked up the side of the road. It was easier to walk there than the snow-littered sidewalk.

Mrs. Hayford's name was written in block lettering beneath the doorbell. There was something decidedly male about the shape of the letters and he wondered if maybe her son had written them. A son writing his mother's name on the outside of her apartment seemed like the kindest thing Sheridan could think of at that moment, as he pressed the button with his free hand.

In his other arm he held one of the two bags of groceries. He stood there for a good amount of time listening to two people talk outside on the sidewalk. He refused to look, but they seemed to be having an important conversation. Occasionally they paused and then started up again. "Mrs. Hayford," Sheridan said, when her voice finally emanated from the small box above the button. "This is Mr. Sheridan. We were worried about you. You never called."

"Mr. Sheridan?" she said.

"You don't have to buzz me in," he explained. "I just wanted to make sure you were fine. I don't think you should have been driving today."

"I know," she said. He wondered if, in her younger days, she had suffered many suitors and had to turn on a slight iciness with them. She seemed to be waiting for him to say something else, to reveal his true motives—or even his true identity.

"I have something for you," he said. "Some vitamins and things. An exercise ball for your bad hand. I think it will help."

This was something that had been in the glove compartment of his truck for over a month. When opening the passenger's side door for the groceries he had remembered it.

"I can just leave them for you," he said.

"Nonsense," she said, and the buzzer rang loudly. He grabbed the door with his free hand, pulled it open, and stepped inside.

There was a carpeted area between the locked outer door and the inner door. A row of mailboxes covered the left wall. A few magazines and scraps of junk mail spattered the floor beneath them. That's where he left the grocery bag.

In the truck he tried to think of a reason not to go home, some other destination. Mrs. Hayford had been that reason, but he took the raisins from the second bag of groceries and peeled back the lid, poked the tinfoil layer open with his thumb. There were at least two layers of protection on everything nowadays. He didn't know what this meant except that maybe there was more danger in the world than...when exactly? When Mrs. Hayford was a child in Cape Breton, floating out in the ocean?

She had not recognized his voice at first, he realized. Maybe she hadn't even placed his name. Not until he mentioned the exercise ball. She had probably been a little afraid.

He wished he had the ball now. Sometimes he took five minutes at the side of the road and squeezed it, or didn't squeeze it at all, just pushed it smaller and held it in that shape firmly, feeling the strength of his own fist around it. Missing that small thing made him feel fragmented, like he had lost something much more important than an old exercise ball. But he couldn't think of a good way to get it back, and, after all, he had wanted to be rid of it anyway.

So he made the steering wheel into a bad substitute—gripping it with both hands—and took a deep breath. This was a different kind of aloneness. He had felt it before, in a room full of people or sometimes with Elizabeth as they pushed themselves through some sexual contortions. There was sharpness there too—like that walk across the high school parking lot in the morning—but something else more complicated. In that first moment it was as if he was looking at a detailed map of himself. It was all laid out before him. In the second—the moment he was living now—well, he was a blur, a smudge.

A couple of kids dressed in jean jackets held snowballs close to their chests, watching his truck as he steered out onto the snow-narrowed street. But they didn't throw them or even raise their arms in the gesture of throwing. They seemed to be waiting for a better target to come along.

Elizabeth met him at the front door. Her eyes were red and her hair was a mess and Sheridan had expected this, although he hadn't expected her to open the door and come halfway down the steps as he walked up. She said, "I found it."

"I know," he said, and then, "Where's Danny?" he asked.

"I put him to bed."

"Two hours early?"

"Jesus," she said. "Let's not talk about Danny. I don't want to think about that."

"You shouldn't think about any of it," he said. "I know I don't. Not usually."

Was this a lie? He wasn't sure.

"Let's talk inside," he said.

"I wouldn't mind talking in the middle of the street," she said.

He was beginning to wonder if he had left it there on purpose. In an odd way maybe he had given it to her. But that was as bad as anything else.

He moved past her and up a few steps. "Inside," he said, making a gesture toward their house. He felt that if they could just make it to the house—if he could just get her in there—then something good might happen.

Ten years, he decided, was a very long time. It had not passed in a flash, the way some people described their marriages, their lives. For a moment he watched the years from an outlying vantage point, like a person looking across a vast landscape. He struggled with the groceries, pushing the door open with his shoulder. From the doorway he could see the dinner dishes set on the table, napkins, silverware, and he wondered if she might have placed these things down after she had stepped from the living room, the TV screen still glowing. Had it crossed her mind to keep a secret of her own, to force a smile and ask him how his day had gone?

"Where is it?" he asked, as she followed him.

"Fuck you," she said. They were inside now, heading across the kitchen. He set the groceries down but only because he would have felt stupid to keep carrying them. He wished they weren't even here. They seemed an indictment of even greater guilt.

"I've been trying to balance things," he explained.

He had thought that when this moment came—he had known that it would come eventually—that he'd become a geyser of truth and remorse. But he didn't feel out of control in the least. He easily could have taken the food out of the bag, placed some in the vegetable drawer in the fridge, the vitamins on a shelf, the red onion and carrot on the chopping block to prepare for dinner.

"Where do you get something like that?" she asked.

"That was a special one," he said, but he couldn't finish.

"That poor girl," she said.

"It's not real," he said, although he had tried so hard and for so long to believe the opposite that he wasn't so sure himself anymore.

"What's not real about it?" she said, voice rising. "Tell me."

"Please," he said, "don't."

For a moment her anger seemed to ebb and she spoke more patiently, her eyes downcast on the kitchen table. Maybe she was thinking about the authenticity of those objects arranged so carefully there, the way they had been every evening for years. "We're going to talk about reality," she said. "Is that it? Is that what we're going to do?"

"No," he said. "I'd rather not do that."

"She *was* real," Elizabeth said.

That same thought had been enough to make him throw the tape away last year, but had also pushed him to retrieve it the next day, reaching deep down into the bottom of the trash beneath the cucumber shavings and coffee grounds. He wondered how long ago the girl had been *that* girl, the kneeling figure she was on the videotape. Ten, fifteen, twenty years. There was nothing in the video to fix it in time or place, just brick walls, a cement floor, the tangled hair in the girl's eyes.

He had sometimes imagined himself in that girl's position. He did not know if this made him more empathetic or if it had simply been a way to deepen his pleasure. Each time she said those words— the words that opened her, that gave up her identity to the men around her—he tried to put himself in that circle too, if only for a few seconds, before the shadows of their weapons flashed downward.

Elizabeth was sobbing. He had expected that too, but not the violence of it. He felt as if he had struck her. He did not ask her, "What now?" or "Are you okay?" He didn't tell her that everything was going to be fine. Those were stupid things to say, of course.

"You," Elizabeth said, "scum."

"Okay," he said.

"Shut the fuck up, you asshole," she said. She was backing away from him, toward the stove, but her arm was coming forward, slashing down. He wondered if Danny would hear.

"Keep going," he said. "More." But none of it hurt.

All he wanted to do was tell her what he had done with his day: the quietness of work, the grocery shopping, and the trip to Mrs. Hayford's house. But all that seemed like a pantomime now, even his gentle questions. Where is your injury? When did you first suffer it? Could you describe it for me using specific language?

THE AUTHOR

Melina Draper

David Crouse is author of the previous story collection *Copy Cats*, which was awarded The Flannery O'Connor Award for Short Fiction in 2005. His short stories have appeared in such magazines as *Quarterly West, Chelsea, The Northwest Review,* and *The Greensboro Review,* while his comic book writing has been anthologized in *The Dark Horse Book of the Dead.* He lives in Fairbanks, Alaska, where he teaches in the MFA Program at The University of Alaska-Fairbanks.